SWORD OF ASGARD

Heroes of Asgard Book Four

S.M. SCHMITZ

Copyright © 2018 by S.M. Schmitz

All rights reserved.

No part of this book may be reproduced in any form or by any electronic or mechanical means, including information storage and retrieval systems, without written permission from the author, except for the use of brief quotations in a book review.

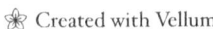 Created with Vellum

CHAPTER ONE

Freyja had helped Havard and Arnbjorg with a curse that forced all of Asgard to forget them so they could protect their family and friends from Odin's wrath. And I'd been stupid enough not to see through her lies and deceptions, to give into her seduction, to *forget* that she'd once called me Havard. Maybe my anger was misplaced, but I *had* to confront her and there was only one person I trusted to help me do it.

When Keira opened her door, I almost lost my resolve altogether. Why hadn't I gone to Agnes? Why would I hurt this Valkyrie, this woman who was apparently as close to a soul mate as we ever got in any world, by telling her the goddess she hated most was harboring secrets of her own? Keira had been hurt enough. And her eyes appeared a bit red and puffy like she'd been crying.

Instead of gushing about Freyja and this curse and admitting just how much Havard had been taking over lately, I put my arms around her and smoothed her hair with one hand as she sighed into my shoulder and hugged me back. I didn't even need to ask her what was wrong. Between losing Tyr and having Thor hospitalized, *everything* felt wrong.

"I'm not sure we can win anymore," she cried. "I was so convinced... good *always* triumphs over evil, right?"

I closed her door with my foot and vacillated between what she needed to hear and the truth. I settled on a compromise. "Evil can win. But the thing about it is that there are more good people in all of our worlds than bad, and even if we can't stop Ninurta, someone will eventually challenge him who can."

"Then why us, Gavyn? Why do we have to be the heroes who sacrifice everything?"

If it weren't so painful, it would have been comical, this complete reversal of roles. How long had it been now since she'd stood in my doorway insisting I was some kind of hero even though I only wanted to get back to my beer and football game? Six weeks? Seven? And there I was, standing in *her* doorway trying to convince her we were the heroes the world needed. "Because if we don't try to stop them, who will?"

Keira pulled back from me and stared at me for what seemed like an insanely long time. Of course, I was just standing there thinking, "*Guess that was the wrong thing to say, dumbass,*" but she was always good at surprising me.

"Promise me something, Gavyn," she demanded.

"If it's something I *can* do, you know I'll promise you anything."

She nodded and said, "You can. It's whether or not you'll be willing."

Where the hell was she going with this?

"No matter what happens," she continued, "kill Ninurta. *That* is the most important goal, even more important than me."

And, apparently, everyone had been keeping secrets from me. How much more did Keira know than she'd ever let on?

"Keira," I started, but she interrupted me, grabbing my shoulders, and her voice took on an urgent, desperate tone.

"*Promise* me," she said again.

But I shook my head and gently removed her hands, holding them in mine. "You know I can't make that promise."

"No," she shouted, yanking her hands out of mine. "You *won't* make this promise. I've lived thousands of years, so why should you have to die?"

I shrugged and told her, "Because it's apparently my destiny. And I've accepted it, so this conversation is over."

Keira crossed her arms and shot me a "Like hell it is" look, so I quickly changed the subject in an effort to distract her. "Look, I need you to take me to Asgard. I have to talk to Freyja."

Her eyes narrowed and she asked, "Why?"

"Because Havard's curse is her handiwork. And I suspect she knows more than she's ever let on."

"I'm going to *kill* her," Keira hissed.

I held up my hands and exclaimed, "Whoa! You've misunderstood. Havard and Arnbjorg *asked* her to place this curse on Asgard in order to protect all of their friends and family. And maybe there's a reason she couldn't tell us she had something to do with it."

Keira eyed me suspiciously for a few moments, obviously forgetting about her insistence I vow to let her die for me, then grabbed my arm and said, "There's only one way to find out."

Even when I *knew* the seemingly instantaneous trip to Asgard was coming, I still found the sudden change in my surroundings disorienting. I blinked against the bright sun and realized I'd never even told Keira *why* Freyja had created the curse in the first place. And now that we were in Asgard, I couldn't point fingers at Odin, even if he were still at the hospital with Thor. He'd had supporters here when the feud with Havard's family began, and I suspected they'd support him again if a civil war broke out.

She immediately began marching toward Freyja's palace, so I hurried to catch up to her while my brain scrambled for some way to tell her Odin was responsible for Havard's death. I mean, clearly Odin was a total douchebag, but he was still her father. "Keira," I said quietly, "you know Asgard isn't safe right now."

She glanced toward me and nodded. "I know we shouldn't speak here of anything you might have learned recently. And I know you'll confirm what I've suspected all along."

"I didn't want this to be true," I admitted. She was my Valkyrie. I didn't want anything to hurt her. I'd die to protect her.

Keira stopped and glanced at me again, her blue eyes reflecting all the pain and regret she was forced to carry silently. But whatever Hallmark moment we would have shared never happened. Freyja spotted us and emerged from her palace, peppering us with questions about her brother then Thor then every other god on Earth. She stood there, wringing her hands nervously as we tried to assure her no one else had died, but this war Ninurta had started had unraveled us all.

"Freyja," I finally sighed, "we're here to talk about Havard."

She blinked at me and her hands stopped moving, and for a second, I thought she would just cross the veil and disappear because she had that deer in the headlights look. But she lifted a shoulder and insisted, "You already know I'm no help."

"I know the origins of the curse," I told her.

She stepped back like she really *was* going to take off on us, so Keira grabbed her arm and pulled her into the atrium of the palace. "We need answers, and you're going to give them to us, even if I have to pry them from you."

Freyja's eyes narrowed and she hissed, "Are you *threatening* me? Do you forget for whom you work?"

"For God's sake, can you two pretend like you don't hate each other for five minutes?" I snapped.

Freyja and Keira glared at each other for a few more seconds before offering me curt nods. I honestly expected them to take out their phones and set the timers like I had *exactly* five minutes to get information from the goddess who'd put a curse on all of Asgard. I figured I might as well start with the most obvious question.

"Why hide your involvement?" I asked. "You lied to us, pretended like you didn't remember Havard either."

Freyja tossed her golden hair over a shoulder and shrugged but averted her gaze. Even the memory of Havard unsettled her, and if I weren't so angry with her, I might have felt sorry for her. How long had she been harboring this unrequited love for a god whose memory she had to carry alone? "I had to," she said. "Partly because everyone would become suspicious of me and treat me like the enemy, and partly because it would endanger everyone I love."

"How?" Keira asked.

"Odin," Freyja replied. "He's more powerful than me and my spell couldn't force him to forget. He doesn't know I had anything to do with it though. He only knows someone helped Havard, and everyone forgot about the feud between them and began acting like nothing happened. As far as the other gods knew, Odin had always been the leader of Asgard."

"So there *was* a war," I whispered, the image of Asgard in charred ruins painfully resurfacing.

"There was a conspiracy," Freyja corrected. "And a handful of battles, but Havard stopped it before all of Asgard could be destroyed. He understood the only thing that could spare his world and everyone he loved was his own life."

Her voice tripped a little, and she turned toward a painting on the wall as if inspecting it, brushing away specks of dust that didn't exist.

"The Sword of Asgard," I pressed. "Where is it?"

She shook her head and kept brushing at the painting. "I honestly don't know. He didn't tell me. He had everything worked out, and only Arnbjorg knew all the details. And she was murdered alongside him."

"By whom?" Keira asked.

Freyja shrugged again. "I don't know that either. And before you ask, I can't lift the curse. Only you can, Gavyn."

"Me?" I may or may not have squeaked.

"By finding the sword."

"Of course," I muttered. Man, my ancestor could be such a dick.

I had a feeling he kinda got a kick out of my frustration with him. Like I said: he could be such a dick.

"What do the others really remember?" I asked. "It seems *everyone* knows more than they've been admitting all along."

"Hey!" Keira protested. "I haven't been lying to you."

"You had your own prophecy that involves me, and I had to figure it out myself."

"Oh, forgive me for wanting to keep you alive," she retorted.

"If you even *think* about taking my place, no way. I'll never forgive you," I snapped back.

"Nobody remembers anything, Gavyn," Freyja assured me. "Only Odin and me. The only thing the others know that you don't are how powerful a god's genes can be. And the more powerful the god, the greater his ability to pass on everything that made him who he was, including his personality and memories."

"So they knew all along I could basically become Havard," I said. They'd *promised* me that couldn't happen, that I'd never lose myself, and I'd stupidly trusted them.

Freyja glanced at Keira before lifting her chin just slightly as if part of her relished that what she was about to say would hurt my Valkyrie. "We all knew that it wouldn't really matter since you weren't going to survive anyway."

"You *bitch*," Keira shouted, stepping toward the goddess as if she intended to settle this ancient hostility once and for all. And even though I agreed with Keira at the moment, I didn't think fighting a war goddess was a good idea, so I grabbed her arm before she could advance further, especially since she didn't even have a weapon.

"Well," Freyja added, "clearly, *Gunnr* wasn't privy to everything we discussed either."

Okay, I totally wanted to fight this goddess, too. Maybe even force her out of Asgard. Burn her palace to the ground. Sure, she'd helped Havard and Arnbjorg all those years ago, but she'd also had a long time to become bitter about it. Her own curse had been the memories no one else shared, so she had to carry her love for a lost god all alone. "I think it would be a good idea for you to stay here," I finally said. "You won't be helping if we're just sniping at each other."

Freyja hesitated but nodded. "All right. But be careful around Odin, Gavyn. If he realizes how much you know, he'll kill you. He's been hoping you'd lead him to the Sword of Asgard, but he won't wait forever, especially if he figures out you can tell the other gods he's behind Havard's murder."

I was about to suggest Keira and I search for the sword while we were there, but Keira's phone rang, and I didn't need the Sword of Prophecy to know we'd be summoned back to Earth for yet another supernatural battle. And like most supernatural battles, we'd have to fight it largely without the aid of the other demigods they'd rounded up since most of them apparently didn't have such powerful ancestors like Joachim and me.

In other words, they kinda sucked at fighting, and we didn't want those poor bastards getting slaughtered.

But apparently, I'd go to my grave being the village idiot my divine friends had come to know, because I found myself thinking the battles should at least be more straight forward from now on with Asalluhi dead and Odin at Thor's bedside.

But I couldn't have been more wrong.

CHAPTER TWO

Keira and I met up with Agnes, Yngvarr, and Ra on the outskirts of Houston, where the Egyptian sun god was pacing and muttering to himself in what may have been Coptic. His son and a group of Egyptian demigods had been spotted in the city, holed up in a hotel near Minute Maid Stadium. Agnes had her feet propped up on the table in their room, smiling and laughing with Yngvarr but as soon as she saw me, she transformed into the ten-thousand-year-old witch and lifted her ancient, shriveled chin in the air.

"Where have you two been?" she scolded. "This is no time for nooners."

"You're one to talk," I shot back.

"Dude," Yngvarr interjected. "Don't suggest we've been fooling around when she's pretending to be Cleopatra's grandmother."

Agnes spun around and turned her withering stare on him. "Cleopatra's grandmother? Why on Earth would I be Greek?"

"Egyptian," I thought I corrected.

But she turned that withering glare toward me and sighed irritably. "The Ptolemaic dynasty was *Greek*, dumbass."

And Havard apparently agreed with her because that seemed right, so I just shrugged and said, "Greek, Egyptian, what's the difference?"

"Do all of you *really* have nothing better to do right now?" Ra snapped.

We shuffled our feet and lowered our heads, mumbling, "Sorry," at the god whose son we'd most likely have to kill soon. Agnes even dropped her disguise and returned to her chair where she cleared her throat and plucked a tablet from the table. "Anhur and a small group of demigods have holed up in a hotel near Minute Maid Park."

"Maybe they're just Astros fans," I suggested before thinking, which was how most of my suggestions were made. Of course, this was also how I'd earned my epithet as the village idiot. I realized too late that baseball season was long over, and everyone in the room quickly reminded me I was a total dumbass.

"My son," Ra said, "is likely our best shot at finding Ninurta and Inanna before they launch yet another disastrous campaign to force humans to worship them through fear. I'm going out there. If the rest of you want to sit in here and argue about dynasties and nooners, I'll go alone."

Ra, the Most Loathsome God in the Universe, stormed out of the room, and honestly, his idea for us to sit around arguing seemed like a good one. I mean, in only two months I'd had every monster imaginable attack me, and I'd fought countless demigods and gods. And if I died before even getting the chance to square off with Ninurta, I was going to be incredibly pissed off.

Havard was apparently far less concerned with Ninurta than Odin, because his smug and punchable face popped into my head, reminding me I actually had *two* mortal enemies to contend with. And besides, Keira was already following Ra, and I couldn't let her go without me. If she were hurt or killed, I'd never forgive myself. I mean, sure, I was going to die soon, too, but I was apparently destined for Valhalla anyway. And I didn't think dead Valkyries got to stay there, so ensuring Keira lived so we could at least be together in Odin's Hall of the Dead was kinda my top priority.

I caught up to her outside the building, which wasn't hard considering she and Ra had frozen in the parking lot, gaping toward downtown Houston. I didn't even want to look. "Dragons?" I groaned.

Keira blinked then slowly tore her attention away from the horizon to blink at me. "What?"

"Are we about to get attacked by poison-filled dragons?"

"What the hell?" Agnes murmured as she stepped outside.

Havard's annoyingly right but obnoxiously arrogant voice piped up, whispering in my mind, "*Perhaps you should pay attention to your surroundings.*"

So, naturally, I told him to shut up and mind his own business, but I said it aloud, which earned me multiple scowls and recommendations that I look into psychotherapy.

Reluctantly, I turned toward the skyline so I could gape at it like my friends. A dull gray had replaced the vibrant colors of the city, and even the baby breath's blue sky had transformed above the colorless buildings. But the strangest aspect of Houston's new visage was the clear line of demarcation. It was like arriving in Oz or something, where we were in the Technicolor part of the movie and the area of the city inside the 610 Loop was still in black and white.

"Um, Agnes? You know all those times I accused you of being the Wicked Witch of the West?"

"Still not a witch, Gavyn, and this isn't my doing," she said.

"But what is it?" Keira asked. "And why would Anhur want to drain the color from a city?"

"To match his soul?" I replied then grinned sheepishly at Ra when Havard reminded me his father was within striking distance.

"This isn't Anhur's doing," Ra said. "It may be for his benefit, but Anhur can't perform spells. He's a war god."

"My father," Keira hissed.

I threw my hands up and hissed back, "Why can't he just stay by Thor's side like a *normal* father?"

"Why would you expect him to do anything *normal*?" Keira demanded.

"Because we could use the break!" I exclaimed.

"You should tell him that," Ra suggested.

"So do we enter the Twilight Zone or not?" I asked.

"We do," Yngvarr said. "How many people work or live inside the Loop? They could be trapped and in danger. And it doesn't change the fact that we need to capture Anhur to find out where Ninurta is."

"Half a million people live there," I answered. "Easily that many work there or are patients at one of the hospitals in the medical district. Probably far more."

"So over a million people," Keira whispered.

I nodded and tried to wrap my mind around that number, but it was impossible. Surely, Odin wouldn't murder over a million people, would he? Yeah, he was a bit of an evil bastard, but *a million people*?

"All right," I relented. "We'll venture in. Maybe Keira will think I'm hotter in black and white and finally sleep with me."

And since we obviously *had* stepped into the Twilight Zone, she just shrugged and said, "Maybe."

Cars on the street in front of us finally seemed to notice the odd lack of color and stopped, people spilling out and pointing and shouting. I had no idea what they thought shouting would accomplish, but not surprisingly, it didn't do a damn thing. The smarter people got back in their cars or never got out in the first place, finding some parking lot or patch of grass to turn around in so they could get as far away from Houston as possible.

By now, most of the world *had* to know the ancient gods had returned, and in their quest for domination and new worshippers, they were willing to destroy cities and murder people so they could teach us all they should be feared. So why the hell *everyone* didn't get back in their cars and leave remained a mystery as we ventured toward the inner city on foot. The gridlock in the streets wouldn't allow us to drive, and occasionally, some well-meaning person would stop us and point to the gray sky like we hadn't noticed the heart of Houston had died. So I'd always tell them, "Don't worry. We're the city painters. We're just running a bit late this morning."

But mostly, no one bothered us, not even the cops who'd shown up and were erecting barricades around the monochromatic portion of the city.

And I really need to wrap up this part of my story since I'm running out of synonyms for "colorless."

As we reached the Loop, yellow police tape stretched across what appeared to be an actual line between the cursed and non-cursed halves of the city. It wasn't *really* a line, but the stark contrast looked like a battle line of some sort, and I suddenly didn't want to cross it. I had flashbacks to the Sumerian labyrinth and those devil dogs hissing my name and backed away from the demarcation.

Keira glanced over her shoulder at me and reached for my hand. "What is it?"

A cop a few hundred yards away spotted us and shouted, "Stay back," then went back to whatever he was doing, which appeared to be nothing more than gawking stupidly at the cursed city. I mean, sure, what else *could* he do? But since I was about to find out what was actually *in* there, I figured I was entitled to take out my anger on some stranger who was completely mystified and way out of his league.

"The last two times I've entered a bizarre or cursed city, I've been confronted with monsters and flooding alleyways and..." I trailed off and pressed my lips together before I could verbalize my experience of watching the first god I'd ever considered a friend die.

Sometimes, I still expected him to come bounding into my room, a platter of burgers in his good hand and a six-pack in a plastic bag slung over his wrist since his prosthetic hand didn't hold weight that well. And thinking about my dead friend *should've* made me want revenge. I should've charged into the accursed inner city, prepared to slaughter any god or demigod who got in my way.

But it only made me sad and defeated before the battle had even begun.

"Tyr," I whispered quietly near her ear. "How many more friends will we lose, Keira? Why can't they live in Valhalla so we *know* they're okay?"

Keira looked around but Agnes, Yngvarr, and Ra had already stepped inside the gray city and were waiting for us out of earshot. "You have the key to discovering what you need to know inside of you. Use it."

Now, this sounded suspiciously like a riddle, and we'd already established why posing riddles to *me* was an epically bad idea. So instead of an "Aha!" moment, I just squinted at her and said, "The only thing inside me is half a day old pizza, but don't judge. I offered you a slice."

Keira held up her hands and said, "I'm judging because you ordered pineapples and sausage on it, and that is seriously the most disturbing thing I've learned about you yet, which is really saying something. And why are we even talking about pizza right now? I obviously wasn't referring to your breakfast."

"Keira," I sighed. "When are you going to learn cryptic doesn't work on me? Do you *honestly* think my cluelessness is just an act?"

"Your cluelessness, no. But you're not stupid either. Since we *are* in a hurry though, I'll point out the obvious: Havard. You just told me he's more and more... vocal. Get him to reassure you about Tyr's fate."

"Oh," I said, like that really should've occurred to me, and it really *should* have but let's face it: you're not at all surprised.

"*All right, you heard her, asshole,*" I told him. "*Reassure me or figure out how to get resurrected and come fight your own damn battles.*"

"*Technically, Gavyn, this is* your *battle.*"

"Oh, shut up," I snapped aloud.

Keira raised an eyebrow at me so I waved her on and said, "They're waiting on us, and I'm kinda worried about what Agnes might do to Yngvarr if we don't get over there."

"I'm pretty sure you're the only one who's worried," she said. "And I'm pretty sure Yngvarr is looking *forward* to whatever Agnes plans on doing to him."

I cringed and wagged a finger in her direction. "Don't ever say anything like that again."

I lifted the yellow tape so she could walk beneath it and held my breath as I stepped over the literal battle line. I looked down at my hands, flipping them over to see if I were really all Cary Grant-ish now, but my hands still looked normal to me. Keira looked me over quickly, flashed me a mischievous smile, and said, "Still in high-def color. Guess you're out of luck."

And while *we* were still in color, the city around us most certainly wasn't, but stranger yet, a voice—most likely a recording being played on some emergency broadcast—kept repeating, "This is an emergency. Stay inside. Keep all doors and windows locked and sealed. This is an emergency. Stay—"

"Um..." I stammered. "Anyone want to take a stab at why we couldn't hear this annoyingly loud announcement three feet away?"

"Twilight Zone," Yngvarr said smartly.

"Vacuum?" Agnes guessed.

"Haven't we suggested vacuums before?" I asked. "And established we'd all die, and I don't *think* I'm dead. But I'm pretty sure you've been dead for like five thousand years, so it probably doesn't affect you."

Agnes flipped me off before getting Ra's attention. "Any ideas?"

"None," he said. "But whatever's going on here, we can't combat it. We just have to continue on to the hotel and hope Anhur is still there *and* that his capture or death will lift Houston's curse."

We let Ra lead our way, not because he knew Houston better than me, although to be fair, most of the times Hunter and I had come to Houston, we hadn't remained sober very long, but simply because it was his son we were after. And it just seemed like the respectful thing to do.

As we turned onto a different city block, Ra suddenly stopped and put his hands on his hips. "I did *not* sign up for this," he muttered.

"What?" we all asked at the same time.

Ra stepped back so we were all standing side-by-side, and for the first time, we were able to see what had forced him to stop.

At the end of the block, a monster that would give the devil dogs a run for their money awaited us. His upper body was that of a man, albeit a large, steroidal man, while his lower body was the thick, elongated tail of a serpent. His tail slowly unfurled and he crossed his arms, scowling at us like *we* were the trespassing freaks of nature.

"Ra's right," I decided. "I didn't sign up for this either. Let's go home."

"Home?" the snake man hissed. "This is your home now. And you won't be leaving it again."

CHAPTER THREE

I grunted in the serpent man's direction and complained, "I *really* wish these mutants would stop talking to us. That's so much more disturbing than trying to figure out their parentage."

"Gavyn," Keira sighed. "*What?*"

I pointed my sword at the serpent man and said, "Half snake, half human. How did he get that way? I mean, somebody *seriously* thought it was a good idea to fool around with a *snake*? Remind me again why you gods ended up with all the supernatural powers when you're out there making... *that*." I wiggled my sword just in case they'd forgotten we'd been confronted with a giant snake man.

"Gavyn, stop talking," Agnes begged.

"It's time," the snake man hissed. "Step forward and learn your fate."

So, naturally, I cocked an eyebrow at him and ordered *him* around. "You slither forward and learn *yours*."

"This *is* my fate," the snake man answered. "Condemned here for eternity. And you, Gavyn, shall meet your destiny—"

"Whoa," I interrupted. "Who talks like that? 'Shall meet

your destiny?' You sound like you're reading from a really bad script. And which of your parents was the perv? I'm guessing your dad. But was he a perverted human or a perverted snake?"

"Gavyn, I'll bring you to meet your destiny myself if you don't shut up," Agnes warned.

The snake man lifted his human torso higher and stuck his chin in the air like he couldn't *believe* we had no idea who he was or who his parents were. Even Havard's usually obtrusive—and admittedly useful—extensive mythological database left me scratching my head. Not literally, of course, since I had a sword in one hand and a shield in the other, although inadvertently stabbing someone in the face because I was acting like a dumbass *did* seem like something I'd do.

"Gavyn," Keira whispered, "snap out of it."

"I'm snapped," I lied.

I was pretty sure even the snake man rolled his eyes at me.

"I am King Minos," the snake man who was apparently named King Minos said. "And you may not pass if you refuse to learn your eternal punishment."

"I don't like the sound of *any* of that," I replied. "What if we just kill you instead?"

"Minos," Ra breathed. "Oh, my God. I know where we are."

"Houston," I slowly reminded him. "Did you hit your head on the way over or something?"

Yngvarr shook his head and gestured toward Minos. "He means he knows where Odin wants us to be, what we're about to reenact."

I groaned and began to question if the people in the cursed part of the city *really* needed saving or if we could just skip yet another reenactment of deadly plagues and animal invasions and fiery hail. Surely, Anhur would eventually get bored and venture out of the Loop, and we could just grab him without having to relive the Plagues of Egypt.

"This may actually be *worse* than reliving the Plagues of Egypt," Ra told me. "Because I'm pretty sure we're in Hell."

"Houston," I corrected again. "But pretty close."

"If we end up needing a sacrifice, I know where we're starting," Agnes muttered.

So I nodded and shot back, "Because no one wants a million-year-old witch."

"I think," Keira sighed, "Ra is referring to Dante's Hell. Any chance one of you actually remembers this poem though?"

"It's been a few centuries since I read it," Ra answered.

I stuffed my shield under an arm so I could pull my phone from my pocket, but not surprisingly, Hell had no reception or Wi-Fi connectivity at all. "Looking up that whole circles of Hell thing is out," I sighed.

"Um, maybe King Minos will just tell us what we're about to encounter," Yngvarr said.

"Don't count on it," Minos retorted.

"Serpent men are assholes," I mumbled loud enough for this particular serpent-man-asshole to hear.

"If you were stuck to a giant snake's body, you'd probably be an asshole, too," Yngvarr said helpfully.

Then Agnes, just as helpfully, added, "You make it sound like Gavyn's not already an asshole."

"Stop saying 'asshole,'" Keira scolded. "This story is supposed to be PG-13."

Okay, she didn't really say that, but since it *is* supposed to be PG-13, I'll skip the rest of this conversation.

We carefully approached Minos, whose long tail coiled beneath his human torso, lifting him higher yet again so that he towered above us. He crossed his arms over his bare chest and scowled at me—not at us, but *me*, which I really should've been used to by now—and said, "You shall be condemned to the Ninth Circle where only the treacherous go."

"Treacherous?" I repeated. "Hey, I'm a lot of things, but I'm not a traitor. *Or* a cheat. Hell, I had a chance to score with Morgan Brinley in high school, but I didn't because I was still seeing—"

"Gavyn," Keira groaned.

My reputation had clearly preceded me, because with all of us distracted by my big mouth, Minos was able to attack. Somehow, he'd produced his own sword and shield and he lunged toward me, frighteningly fast for a dude stuck to a snake's body. I only avoided decapitation by falling, which gave me enough time to raise my shield and deflect his second strike. I heard the clinking of someone's sword against metal and assumed Minos's reinforcements had arrived, but Agnes shouted, "His scales are impenetrable!"

Of course they were.

I rolled away from Minos so I could get to my feet, and he whipped his body around to attack Keira. By the time I was upright again, she'd deflected his advance and tried to impale him with her sword, but go figure—his scales were impenetrable on his other side, too.

That meant there was only one way to kill him: we had to strike the human half of him. Fortunately, my Egyptian ally, who was unforgivably good-looking even when battling a freakish snake man, was kinda smart and had already figured out our best shot at getting past Minos. He fired an arrow at the king's chest, but Minos blocked it with his shield.

Agnes raised her bow and began to fire arrows at him, too, while Yngvarr handed Keira a bow and quiver. Everyone except Ra had been around during my archery lessons, so they didn't even bother arming me with a bow. Instead, I used my magical shield to protect them while they turned Minos into a serpentine porcupine.

By the way, the only thing that could have made Minos more nightmarishly disgusting was if he *could* hurl quills at us. But even with a chest full of arrows, the damn guy wouldn't die. Now, I'm not saying it was Havard who realized just how difficult our trek through Dante's Hell was going to be, because maybe my genius had progressed to the point that I was able to have entire conversations with myself, during which... okay, yeah, it was Havard.

"You can't kill him because he's already dead."

Great. Another undead creature. Granted, Minos didn't seem interested in drinking our blood, so he was still a better adversary than Mesopotamian vampires, but *come on*. Sending ghost freaks after us just seemed like cheating, and one of the circles of this place should definitely be for cheaters like Odin.

I sensed Havard growing frustrated with me, so I silently snapped, *"Then tell me what to do, jagweed!"*

His frustration morphed into confusion, but the giant snake king was still attacking us, so I didn't have time to engage in the etymology of modern television profanity. When Havard's voice fell silent, and not just because he was trying to figure out what "jagweed" meant, I assumed he didn't have a clue how to get past Minos either and I was on my own. I would've hurled a few more colorful and totally stolen from pop culture curse words at him, but Minos was starting to get cocky knowing we couldn't harm his serpentine lower half or reach his humanoid torso and head.

He took his time with us now, keeping his upper body far above us, as he plucked the arrows from his chest and flicked them away like splinters. And now that Havard had decided to become useless again, I had to figure out how to vaporize this bastard without a dead god of war's help.

As my allies tried to slow him down again, I actually *did*

have a brilliant idea, but I'd need Havard's help, after all. "*What killed Minos in his story?*" I asked.

I could feel Havard's memories tumbling through my mind as he attempted to pull that particular story to my consciousness. Or maybe it was all really just me talking to myself and working through problems with the aid of Havard's memories, but I hardly had time for an existential crisis.

"*Boiling water*," Havard exclaimed. "*The daughters of King Cocalus poured boiling water on him while he was bathing.*"

I actually had to stop deflecting Minos's arrows in order to complain aloud, "That is the dumbest way to die in the entire history of murders *ever*."

"Gavyn," Keira screamed, "shield!"

I raised my enchanted shield just in time to block the arrow Minos had launched at my face. That didn't seem like a particularly pleasant way to die, but it definitely beat being *boiled alive*.

I scooted back toward Ra and whispered, "Is there water around and would you be able to get it boiling?"

Ra released his arrow, which was as ineffective as all the others, and offered me a small nod. "There's a fire hydrant at the corner, but how would we collect the water so I could produce a fire beneath it?"

I hurriedly answered him before Havard could butt in and take credit for my idea. "Can you get it boiling from within the pipes? Once it's as hot as you can make it, we can lure Minos over to the hydrant and I'll break the valve so we can boil this bastard to death. To re-death?" I shook my head and added, "Hell, I don't care, just do it!"

I left his side before he could even agree or argue with me that my ill thought out plan couldn't possibly work. And he probably would've been right. I got Keira's attention then nodded toward the hydrant. Somehow, she seemed to understand what I needed to do because she began taunting Minos while taking careful steps backwards, bringing our arrogant dead King of the Freaks closer and closer to what I *hoped* would be the same kind of scalding water that had killed him the first time.

Yngvarr and Agnes pursued him from the opposite side so that he couldn't escape—not quickly anyway—while Ra concentrated on the water running beneath the city. Yngvarr and Agnes didn't even know what we were doing or why, but it didn't matter. That was just the kind of faith they'd placed in me.

Keira and I had backed ourselves into a narrow space between a building and Houston's omnipresent construction barriers. We had nowhere left to go, and Minos knew it, too. He laughed and raised his bow, so I pulled Keira closer to me and covered her with my shield. But with my view obstructed, I didn't see Minos's tail whip around until it was too late.

That strong, powerful tail knocked the enchanted shield from my hand, leaving us completely vulnerable and defenseless. Minos's face seemed to darken as he narrowed his eyes at me. He'd won. And he was going to relish this victory.

I shoved Keira behind me, fully intending to use my body as a shield, but Ra shouted, "Gavyn, now!"

Instead of struggling with a freakishly strong Valkyrie who still stubbornly refused to let me sacrifice myself for her, I raised my sword and knocked off the valve on the fire hydrant, sending a steaming spray of water toward the serpent man barricading our entrance into Hell.

Ra, Agnes, and Yngvarr ran to avoid being burned alive by what seemed more like lava than water. Panting, Ra placed his hands on his knees as sweat dripped from his forehead, and we watched Minos writhe for a few moments before he screamed and began to break apart like he himself was only steam from the boiling water assaulting him.

"I can't believe this worked," Ra murmured.

"You cut through a fire hydrant with a *sword?*" Yngvarr asked me.

I shrugged. "It's one of your supernatural swords, so I guess godly metals are way stronger than mortal metals."

"I don't think mortal metals are a thing," Agnes pointed out smartly. "You know, since they were never alive in the first place."

Minos's final screams broke apart just like the final, ethereal remnants of his body. We stood silently for a while, staring at the steaming puddle in the street before I asked the question I really didn't want answered. "Now what? Second Circle?"

"No," Yngvarr sighed. "This *is* the Second Circle. The first was the vacant, gray land known as Limbo. So now, we find out what's in the Third Circle of Hell."

CHAPTER FOUR

I covered my nose with the bottom of my shirt, but it did little to block the putrid smell marking the Third Circle of Hell. A light drizzle fell only a few feet away from us, but since we hadn't crossed circles, we remained dry for now. And whatever fell from the dark gray sky wasn't rain. A sickly yellow, it looked more like phlegm than water and as it collected in the streets, it formed thick green-yellow puddles.

"Can we go around this circle?" I asked.

Yngvarr wrinkled his nose and said, "Doubt it. Maybe we can just run through it?"

A tall figure at the opposite end of the street slipped in the foul slime as he tried to run into the shelter of a nearby building, but otherwise, everyone had the sense to stay indoors. The man struggled to get back on his feet, since the rain apparently acted like glue, so I sighed and cursed my hero genes compelling me to go help the guy.

"Aw, damn it," I sighed again.

Keira followed my gaze, slowly and carefully lifted a foot over one of the yellow puddles in the street, and shot me a farewell look, like we just *knew* this sludge had to be toxic and would kill us on contact. Really, given its smell and appearance, how could it *not* be toxic and fatal on contact? As her foot touched the citrine pool, I may or may not have made a strange squeaking sound. I mean, *somebody* made a squeaking sound but since we were all one stench away from losing our breakfasts, it could've been any of us. And given his track record with Gross Encounters of the Supernatural Kind, I was putting my money on Ra.

But Keira didn't collapse or drop dead or turn into some phlegmy swamp monster. Sure, she made a disgusted face and kept wiping thick, yellow slime off her face, but she was alive and didn't seem to be in any pain. So still holding the edge of my shirt over my face, I stepped into the Third Circle of Hell.

Impossibly, the smell was worse here even though I'd only walked two feet. A cross between Bourbon Street at 3:00 in the morning and a poorly kept pigpen, I wondered aloud what those condemned to this circle could've possibly done to deserve this.

"I'd say child abusers, but they deserve far worse than this," Keira said, occasionally gagging when the wind shifted and blew more vile air toward us.

Ra nodded, retched a bit but managed to keep the contents of his stomach where they belonged and said, "I think it's gluttony."

"Gluttony?" I repeated. "Like overeating? This is a fitting punishment for something most Americans do on a regular basis?"

"When you're gorging yourself all the time while people starve to death all around you, then aren't you kinda responsible for letting those people die?" Keira explained.

As crazy as it seemed, I sometimes forgot my new friends

had been around long enough to witness an aristocracy that cared so little for the masses that their deaths were meaningless to them.

We reached the man who was still struggling to get across the street and into the safety of a building, and Ra and I had to each take an arm and pull him from the ground. The man's eyes were wide and feral, and he was mumbling incoherently. The double-breasted suit he wore suggested he was a businessman, and most likely sane, but the entire world was going to need a mega dose of Xanax and loads of therapy after all the supernatural threats and curses we'd experienced lately.

Agnes tugged on the door to the building where a crowd of people huddled in the lobby, their eyes just as wide and feral as the man's. Nobody rose to help him inside or asked if he were okay or even registered another victim of Odin's depraved mind was joining them. Yngvarr and I glanced at each other, both thinking the same thing: this wasn't normal, even for a group of people in shock.

Odin's curse obviously extended to the humans trapped within the city.

We helped the man onto the floor where he pulled his knees to his chest and rocked slowly back and forth. Several hundred eyes turned away from us and focused on nothing again. "Zombies," Agnes whispered. "He's turned them into zombies."

I nodded and tried to uncurl my fingers, but my body wanted revenge. What if killing Anhur didn't restore these people's personalities? What if the hundreds of thousands of people trapped in Odin's Hell never recovered? This seemed a far worse fate than death.

Unable to help them, we trudged back to the street and reoriented ourselves by glimpsing a small part of the stadium. "If each circle is approximately the same size as the first," I said, "then Minute Maid Park is right in the middle of the ninth, which is where Minos wanted me to go."

Agnes nodded and agreed with me. "We all know it's a trap, but what choice do we have? We've got to capture Anhur even if he *can't* tell us where Ninurta is hiding as that may be the only way to lift the curse on this city and free these people."

"What makes you so sure killing Anhur will work?" Yngvarr asked.

Agnes shrugged. "Because Odin wouldn't stay here. He probably placed the curse, tied it into Anhur's survival, and returned to Thor's bedside. He needs us to still believe he's on our side so Gavyn will lead him to the Sword of Asgard."

Ra rubbed his chin and wiped sticky slime from his eyes. "And if Anhur is killed without the curse lifting, we'd get suspicious as to who's controlling it. With Asalluhi dead, there aren't many gods capable of this kind of magic."

"Then let's walk," I suggested. "We're already covered in butt juice, so—"

"Gavyn," Keira groaned. "If you ever say that again, I *will* reconsider not only my feelings for you, but our entire friendship."

Yngvarr nudged my arm and whispered, "I thought it was a pretty apt description actually."

I snorted and wanted to tell him it would definitely explain the smell, but I was afraid Keira wasn't bluffing. So we walked mostly in silence since none of us wanted to open our mouths more than absolutely necessary. It was one thing to be subjected to this smell, but I was pretty sure any of this shit-rain landing in my mouth would kill me from sheer revulsion.

I estimated we were about halfway across the Third Circle when I heard the low, throaty growls echoing between two buildings. Our slow trek through the sticky street came to a sudden stop, immediately quashing any hope that I'd only imagined those sounds. "Please don't be devil dogs," I murmured to myself.

"Um," Ra murmured back, "I think I remember who guards the Third Circle."

"If you tell me it's those devil dogs—" I started, but two things happened at once, interrupting me before I could even threaten a powerful sun god who was supposed to be on my side anyway. And, yeah, maybe *that's* why Minos had told me I belonged in the Ninth Circle of Hell with all the other traitors, but in my defense, he *was* the Most Loathsome God in the Universe *and* those devil dogs scared the shit out of me.

Anyway, the first thing that happened was that the low growls echoed again, only this time accompanied by the clicking of sharp nails on pavement, meaning whatever monster was out there was getting closer. And the second interruption was Ra telling me, "Not just a devil dog. *The* devil dog. The original Hellhound."

Now, I had no idea who or what he was talking about, so Havard decided to shove an image in my head that may have made me yelp and slip in the putrid sludge. And if I did, Agnes would've caught my arm and steadied me. I turned to her and demanded, "What the hell *is* that thing?"

"Cerberus," she answered quietly. "And no stories exist about its death. I think our only option here will be to outsmart it."

"Well, I'm screwed," I announced. I kinda expected *someone* to argue with me, but instead, they each nodded and held their weapons ready to fight the Hellhound of Hades.

It rounded the corner of the building and even Havard cringed. Not literally, of course, since the dude didn't have a body and all, but that dog was one ugly bastard. With three heads, a serpent's tail, and what may have been random snakes protruding from its body, this creature was like some bad CGI nightmare from a low budget 90s horror movie. And that description may *seem* really specific, but come on—I was battling freaks of nature that weren't supposed to exist, so I'd earned the right to bestow stupidly specific descriptions on them.

One of its heads turned toward me, its blood red eyes narrowing, its teeth bared with some of the same bile-yellow slime oozing from the corners of its mouth. The eyes on its middle head fixed on Keira, who looked far less worried about this literal beast of Hell than I was. "Okay, any guesses as to what kills a three-headed canine demon?" I asked.

Ra cringed, shook his head, and lifted his bow, ready to fire an arrow at one of Cerberus's heads, but Havard suddenly panicked and I shouted, "Don't!"

Ra hesitated and everyone stared at me, dumbfounded by my outburst. Even Cerberus had momentarily stopped growling so he could focus all six eyes on me, that vaporous stench clouding from his panting mouths. But Cerberus's surprise wore off first, and he used our temporary immobility to attack. Even though I had all of his memories at my disposal, Havard still thought he had to yell, "*Don't use your sword! Iron won't hurt him and it'll only piss him off.*"

I wanted to shout back, "I know that, dumbass," followed by, "What the hell am I supposed to do then?" But Cerberus leapt at my face, and I'm pretty sure I've clearly established my feelings on having any body part ripped off. I dropped my sword so I could use both hands to grip and swing my shield at the snarling, odiferous head closest to me. And for the first time since getting Odin's enchanted shield, I was *really* glad it was made from wood. The combination of its enchantment and the force behind my swing knocked Cerberus nearly thirty feet to my left. He slid a ways along the slime that had accumulated like sleet and shook each of his heads as he clawed at the pavement, trying to get back on his feet so he could attack again.

"You can't use iron on him," I told my allies. "Grab anything non-metallic just to be on the safe side and we'll have to hope we can just beat the bastard to death."

"How—" Agnes started but apparently changed her mind when she realized I wouldn't have answers anyway, other than, "Because Havard said so."

Cerberus growled, which was actually like three monstrous dogs growling, and attacked again. I jumped in front of my friends, swinging my shield at one of his heads, but this time, I missed. Cerberus was obviously a little smarter than normal dogs, because he'd already learned my sole strategy for defeating him and figured out how to thwart my blows by lowering all three heads and crouching beneath my swing then springing up once my shield passed safely above his heads. Well, *almost* safely above his heads. I did manage to graze an ear, which seemed to stun him a bit thanks to the enchantment, but Cerberus was in the perfect position to knock me to the ground and eat my face or use those insanely long claws to rip open my chest.

I didn't have time to panic. Cerberus's flanks rippled as he prepared to launch himself at me, and I could only think, "*This is also a totally unacceptable way to die.*"

But those rotting fangs and sickle-like claws never dug into my flesh. Keira appeared beside me, holding a plastic pipe, although I couldn't imagine where she'd found it in the middle of a Houston street turned Third Circle of Hell. But even without the enchantment of my shield, Keira's plastic pipe knocked Cerberus back onto the street, giving us a few much-needed seconds to regroup.

Ra and Agnes had finally returned with their own non-metallic weapons—a wooden mace that Ra must've retrieved from his own world, while Agnes clutched a blown glass turquoise vase. I grunted at her, but she cut me off before I could even ask her what the hell she thought she could accomplish with a *vase*. I mean, I told her to grab a non-metallic weapon, but that was seriously the best object she could find?

"Trust me," Agnes said. "Beat him down then figure out how to pin him to the ground."

Since Cerberus was already on his feet, we had no choice but to trust Agnes as she'd asked. With three of us now, we each targeted one of the heads, and Cerberus did a rather impressive backwards summersault but landed at an awkward angle, allowing us to bludgeon him before he could rise again. But go figure: Hellhounds weren't so easy to kill. The bastard was actually shaking us off when I heard the glass vase shatter against the pavement and Agnes shouting, "Pin him down!"

So I did the only thing I could think of to pin a three-headed serpent dog from Hell to the ground: I jumped on his back. Ra and Keira threw themselves on Cerberus as well, straining against the massive muscles of this beast, as Agnes skidded through the slime, dropped to a knee and in one smooth, swift motion, sliced open one of the Hellhound's throats. Dark blood, so deeply red it almost appeared black, mixed with the vile yellow mucus that coated the street, and I turned my head so I wouldn't have to see the sticky combination of whatever was falling from the sky and whatever was falling from this freakish hybrid monster.

I still heard the flesh being ripped open on Cerberus's second throat followed by his guttural protests, and my nose instinctively wrinkled in disgust. But the Hellhound grew weaker and struggled less against the weight on his body. By the time Agnes slit his third throat, that oddly disturbing serpent tail stilled and the snakes on his body, which must've been ornamental since not one of them tried to bite me, fell limply against the mutant's side.

None of us moved for a few moments, waiting to see if this was only a trick or if we'd actually managed to kill a beast not even Heracles had slain. Granted, *killing* Cerberus hadn't been part of his Twelfth Labor but still. When the serpent dog didn't move or breathe, we slowly rose and stared at its corpse, covered in blood and yellow sludge, and I shuddered and backed away from it.

"Remind me again why it's so important for us to capture Anhur?" I said.

"Because I know my son," Ra answered. "And if he's conspired to curse an entire city, he won't be content with its enslavement through a spell. He'll slay the entire city just to satisfy his lust for violence."

I blinked at the sun god then snapped, "Dude, what the hell is wrong with your progeny?"

"Don't use big words," Agnes warned. "We've told you that freaks us out."

"More than godly offspring slaughtering millions of people?"

Agnes just shrugged and retrieved her sword from its mystical hiding place. "I'm used to dealing with evil gods. I'm *not* used to you acting like you have any intelligence whatsoever."

Keira *almost* smiled but seemed to remember what still lay ahead of us. Her expression hardened again as she took as deep a breath as possible in this fetid wasteland and said, "The Fourth Circle should only be a couple more blocks. And we should expect each one to become more and more difficult the closer we get to Anhur."

"Man, I wish I had the Sword of Asgard," I muttered. With its power, I could easily wipe out whatever awaited us in each circle. But Havard had fallen mysteriously quiet again, hiding from me and my accusations that he could help us now by just telling me where his damn sword was or who had it.

But when he didn't resurface, my suspicion that I'd had all along seemed confirmed.

Havard himself had no idea where the Sword of Asgard was hidden.

CHAPTER FIVE

Stepping into the Fourth Circle was actually a huge mood booster because the horrific stench suddenly ended. I could look over my shoulder and literally *see* a wall of the foulest air in the history of the universe. And bonus: the sticky yellow rain ended as well.

The Fourth Circle was filled with giant stones and boulders that we had to carefully weave our way between. Like the first three circles, this one appeared to be largely deserted as well, and I'd just started wondering where all of the Houstonians were when we heard the muffled moans of people in torment.

I whipped around like they'd magically appeared behind me, and my dumbass was actually a little surprised when the rock-filled street remained free of suffering humans. The sounds continued though, and we were each convinced those moans were coming from different directions.

"Should we split up?" Ra asked.

"No," Agnes answered. "We continue on to reach the Fifth Circle. The only way we can save everyone in Houston is to end this curse."

As usual, Agnes made sense but my demigod genes protested loudly with each step through the rocky landscape, particularly when the tormented cries grew more urgent and desperate and seemed so much closer. And these cries didn't sound zombified like those poor people trapped in the stench of the Third Circle. They sounded like people in pain.

We'd just reached what appeared to be a mountain of limestone and cinderblock when the sounds converged, narrowing into a single, echoing groan rising from a pit that had formed in what used to be a pay-to-park lot. I immediately approached the giant hole in the ground, but Keira grabbed my arm and pulled me back before I could peer over the ledge.

"Haven't you learned yet that everything is a trap with these gods?" she scolded.

"Yeah," I said, "but I also learned early on that they're willing to kill innocent people to force our hand. So if there are people trapped down there, I'm going to save them."

Ra took a deep breath and nodded. "I'll go with you."

Yngvarr looked like he was about to volunteer as well, but Agnes stepped in front of him and ordered, "Stay here with Keira in case anyone attacks us from up here. I'm going with them."

But we all knew what she was *really* saying was more like, "Whatever's happening down there scares the shit out of me, and I'd rather die than let you get hurt again." Which would have been really sweet if my gag reflex hadn't kicked in, forcing me to retch loudly and prompting everyone else to flip me off.

Agnes and Ra smiled a bit *too* slyly at me and she said, "Heroes first. I mean, it's literally in your job description."

"Remind me to look for another job," I retorted. And for good measure, added, "And how to kill witches if we ever get out of Dante's Hell."

Agnes nodded and pointed her sword toward the pit. "They'll both be on my to-do list. Now go ahead: jump in."

And really, I couldn't stand around pretend-threatening my friends all day, so I carefully inched to the lip of the pit and glanced inside. My stomach dropped, and my throat tightened so I couldn't call for Ra or Agnes to hurry. I could do nothing for a few moments but stare, shocked and sickened, at the mortals weighted down by huge stones, some of which were wrapped with rough rope around their necks so that any movement could result in asphyxiation.

But worst of all, Odin apparently didn't share Ninurta's reservations about hurting children because it wasn't only adults trapped in the pit, unable to move, unable to cry for help, fated to die this slow, cruel death. And as soon as Keira learned there were children trapped below, she would abandon her watch and we actually *did* need them to protect us from threats on the ground while we went into the pit to free these people. But I couldn't take this from my Valkyrie, this woman whose heart longed so deeply for children of her own that she'd risked her life, risked *everything* to save one so long ago.

"Agnes," I finally croaked out. "Take Keira's place. Send her with me."

"Why?" Agnes asked, moving toward the edge of the pit to join me in my horror, but I stopped her by yelling, "Damn it, Agnes, just do it!"

She blinked at me but lowered her sword and glanced over her shoulder. "Gavyn needs you, Keira. And this is the end game. We all need to be listening to him now."

I'm not gonna lie: hearing her talk like that, like I was the only guy in the world who could save it, made me cringe and want to run away from this responsibility, from what *had* to be a massive mistake because I was no great hero. Sure, I could pass for some sidekick maybe, but a Perseus? No way.

They'd gotten the wrong guy. Clearly. Hadn't I demonstrated that through my stupidity alone?

But Keira joined me and stared into the pit, sucking in a quick, harsh breath before sheathing her sword and reaching for my hand. "Lower me in," she demanded. "I'll cut them loose then we'll pull them out."

Ra had braved looking into the pit as well and was rubbing his perfectly sculpted chin as he thought. Have I mentioned I *really* didn't like this guy? I mean, sure, he was considerate and moral and compassionate and all that, but no man or god had any right to be *that* much of a threat to every single heterosexual male on the planet. And that was assuming Ra wasn't bisexual, in which case, he had no right to be that much of a threat to every adult *male* on the planet.

As if sensing my thoughts had wandered off again, Keira snapped, "Gavyn, lower me into the pit!"

Ra let his hand fall and added, "Me, too. I'll start moving boulders to the wall to help people get high enough for you to reach them. I can carry the youngest kids out on my back."

I followed his gaze and for the first time, noticed a cluster of children who couldn't be more than two or three, just as weighted down by stones as the rest of the poor people trapped within. "Keira," I breathed. I hadn't intended her name to be a breath, but I felt like I'd been body slammed by the Goliath I'd already killed, and a zombie Goliath was probably a *lot* heavier and stronger than a normal Goliath on account of devouring all those brains.

But Keira still heard me and reached for my hand so I could help her descend the thirty feet into the pit. Jumping in was too dangerous an option considering all of the jagged rocks that littered the ground, so I would have to carefully lower her into a relatively stone-free area that couldn't have been more than a few square feet.

But the guardian of the Fourth Circle had no intention of

allowing any of us to rescue those people. "And where," a voice oddly both masculine and feminine said, "do you think you'll bring these prisoners?"

Like the initial moaning itself, the voice seemed to originate from everywhere and nowhere, from above and below and none of us could find its source. But when our mystery voice spoke again, it sounded closer and Havard decided to wake his lazy ass up and help us. "*Plutus,*" he said. "*The Greek god of wealth. He's fickle and unpredictable. Be careful here, Gavyn.*"

"Because otherwise, I would have been careless and reckless in my face-off with a Greek god?" I snapped aloud, which earned me a confused look from Keira, but I ignored it because now that I'd thought about Havard's warning, I grinned sheepishly to myself and added—silently, this time—"*Okay, yeah, that's fair.*"

Keira stood beside me but seemed conflicted about whether she should stay on the ground to fight Plutus or jump into the pit and risk impalement on one of those sharp boulders. She must've decided to stay and fight because her sword suddenly glinted in the dim, dying sunlight and she yelled, "Did you do this to those children?"

Plutus, who had finally entered our line of sight, simply smiled and spread his hands like he was *proud* of his handiwork here.

Now, I'd obviously killed gods before, but something told me Plutus could be trickier to beat, and that something was probably called "Havard." And maybe that was the key: we would have to trick him in order to defeat him. And, okay, yeah, that was definitely Havard cluing me in on what we'd need to do, but I think I still deserve most of the credit since I was the one who had to *take* his advice and actually execute his plan.

I backed slowly toward the pit until my heels kissed the

edge, sending broken chunks of asphalt into what was essentially a quarry. Miscalculations could be painful and deadly.

"To answer your question," I said to Plutus, "I think I'll bring these people to you."

I spun around and jumped. All of my allies screamed my name like I'd just sacrificed myself to an angry volcano god—against whom, by the way, I would've drawn a hard line against fighting—but I'd surveyed this pit before Plutus showed up and knew where the few rock-less areas were. Sure, I could easily miss, but sometimes, apparently, being a hero required a bit of recklessness.

The impact of landing on a hard surface after a thirty-foot drop still twisted my ankle painfully, but I forced myself to rush to the nearest prisoner and cut the tether around her neck. Behind me, I heard someone else landing followed by her soft grunt. I'd expected Keira to follow me without even knowing my plan. I would've done the exact same thing for her. And I'd also expected her to run to the youngest children first. My Valkyrie didn't disappoint me.

Havard and I were banking on Plutus's greed besting him, compelling him to follow us into the pit to protect what he regarded as his property. And that bastard didn't disappoint me either.

I heard him land just as I cut the tether from a second prisoner and twisted around on one knee, holding my shield above us and just in time, too. The blade of Plutus's sword smashed into the shield's enchantment, sending the Greek god stumbling backward toward a mound of jagged rocks. He caught himself before he could be impaled on one particularly nasty looking stalactite-esque boulder.

But Havard quickly reminded me that was exactly why we —I mean, *I*—had jumped into this pit. I dropped my sword onto the ground so I could use both hands to swing my shield at the Greek god's face. One corner caught him beneath his chin, and he stumbled again but still didn't fall onto the sharp rocks. But Keira had caught on to my strategy and put her own sword away to lift a surprisingly large and heavy stone, which she threw at Plutus as if it were only papier-mâché.

The god of wealth sidestepped the large rock, and it smashed against the pile of jagged boulders behind him, sending shards of sharp splinters into the god's translucent skin. Beside me, another figure landed, and the bright red blur in my peripheral vision immediately told me Agnes had come up with her own strategy on the ground, most likely placing Ra and Yngvarr in key positions to defend us from above if Plutus's reinforcements arrived while she joined our fight below. And because this *was* Badb, after all, the fearsome war goddess of the Tuatha Dé who was renowned throughout the supernatural world for her prowess in battle, she wasted no time in helping Keira and me back Plutus against the rocks.

Somehow, she'd found Keira's plastic pipe and swung it at Plutus's arm, whose hand still held his sword. The sharp crack as it snapped bones made the Greek god drop his weapon, and I cringed and started to get distracted again by my own revulsion but Havard screamed, "*Now, Gavyn! He has nowhere to go and no weapon.*"

I had to step dangerously close to the Greek god in order to ensure I hit him hard enough that he wouldn't be able to regain his balance, and Keira—my brave and freakishly strong Valkyrie—bought me a few seconds of distraction by hurling another large stone at Plutus's head. While the god attempted to catch the rock since he couldn't sidestep this one, I swung my shield one last time, directly below his rib cage to throw off his center of gravity.

Between the impact of the edge of the shield and its enchantment to forcefully propel all objects away from it, Plutus finally lost his footing and fell backwards, directly into the sharp corners of the massive stones he'd piled around this pit to discourage any escape or rescue attempts. Blood gurgled from his lips as his hand groped his stomach where crimson stains spread quickly across his pale tunic. Keira eyed him for a few seconds as if wanting to ensure he'd truly die before turning on her heels and running back to the children so she could free them first.

Agnes plucked my sword from the ground and confidently approached the dying Greek god. "You don't deserve our mercy, but you'll receive it nonetheless. Because that will always be what separates gods like you from gods like us: our refusal to let anyone suffer, even monsters like you."

And she ran my sword through his heart.

It may have only been my imagination, but I thought the sky above the Fourth Circle of Hell brightened just a little with the Greek god of wealth's death. And for the first time since my prophecy was revealed, I began to wonder if I might get out of this alive, after all.

HAVARD DROPS A BOMBSHELL ON ME

(And if there's some Heaven for gods, I will find him and kick his ass for this.)

We'd watched Astrid grow into the beautiful and intelligent goddess we'd always known she'd become and welcomed several siblings for her along the way. Finn, her uncle, had married and begun his own family, and Yngvarr's arrangement with Badb in which they split their time between Asgard and the Otherworld had worked surprisingly well for them.

Admittedly, my life was filled with so much happiness that there were many times I forgot about Odin's absence and its significance, as well as Freyja's promise to put a spell on everyone we knew in order to save them from Odin's vengeance. I'd reluctantly assumed the role of an interim ruler of Asgard, but not everyone had accepted even this temporary arrangement and tensions would occasionally erupt into brawls that were quickly settled by threats of exile. For the most part, though, Asgard was peaceful and the gods who lived here enjoyed years of not having to worry about incurring Odin's wrath.

But years meant so little in Asgard—only mortals needed to measure time in such a way—so how many years had passed when I found Áki standing in my dining hall with his hands clasped nervously behind his back? He'd grown into a brilliant swordsman with the heart of both a fighter and peacemaker, and I was neither stupid nor blind. I knew why he was here.

We spoke only of trivial occurrences around Asgard until Arnbjorg joined us, and the mood in the room immediately shifted. Áki cleared his throat, but I held up a hand and stopped him before he could ask us.

"Do you remember how you came to live in Asgard?" I said.

"I do," he answered.

We'd never spoken about the death of his family or how I'd ordered his execution as well.

"And do you find yourself missing Midgard?"

My question seemed to surprise him, but he replied, "No, my lord. Asgard is the only home I remember well. And how could anyone not love this place and *want* to call it home?"

I offered him a nod and a smile, because while I'd anticipated his answer, it didn't make what I was about to say any easier. "A time will come, though, that Arnbjorg and I will need you to flee this world with your family, to live among humans in Midgard, to be willing to grow old and die with them as any other mortal there."

"My lord—" he began, but I stopped him again.

"We know you're here to ask for our blessing with Astrid. And we know that she loves you. Arnbjorg and I will one day have to make a tremendous sacrifice to prevent Asgard's destruction, so we need to know you'll be prepared to escape this world without hesitation."

Áki glanced between us and took a deep breath. "And my mother?"

"Gunnr will stay here. Leaving Asgard with you would

only make things worse for your family. Valkyries are forbidden to live in Midgard."

The young man seemed to consider this, our insistence that he flee with Astrid and their children, that he leave the woman who'd raised him behind in a world that could become dangerous.

"Why are you so certain that Asgard can't be saved?" he finally asked. "You have more support here than Odin."

"And that," I explained, "is precisely why I'm certain there can be only one solution. Odin will one day return with an army of strange gods, preferring to end this world rather than see it in my hands."

"Then Asgard is condemned to be ruled by a despot forever?" he asked.

"No," I answered. "It is fated to be ruled by someone greater than I."

For the first time since joining us, Arnbjorg spoke, telling the boy who would become our son, "You and I were never meant to live among the gods, and yet, here we are, destined to play a role in Asgard's salvation."

"My lady?" Áki whispered.

"Astrid will marry you, and together, you will have a daughter whose son will one day save both worlds by making the same sacrifice Havard and I are prepared to make. You will tell your daughter that Fate has honored our family and that Havard and I will guide them. They'll suffer nothing alone."

I took Arnbjorg's hand and brought it to my lips, knowing how much time we still had but how little it seemed.

"Oh," I said, "one more thing. Badb will retrieve my sword from the god who takes it in exchange for sparing your lives, and she will bring it to you. Give it to your daughter. Her son will one day need it not only to save our worlds but to avenge our deaths."

Áki seemed to consider this for only a moment before standing taller and promising, "I will do exactly as you've asked, my lord. I will ensure Astrid and our children are safe, whether we're here in Asgard or biding our time in Midgard. And I hope I'm still alive to witness my grandson causing the entire house of your murderer to crumble around him."

CHAPTER SEVEN

I stopped in the middle of the street just inside the Fifth Circle. A wide swamp stretched before us, its surface dotted with people stumbling and slipping as they attempted to reach a shore that appeared to move farther away with each precarious step. It should've registered with me how odd it was that they were walking *atop* the water of the slimy swamp, but my thoughts had become fixated on the memory Havard had just sucker punched me with.

Agnes nudged me, but my feet refused to cooperate. My *mother* was Havard's *granddaughter*? I'd always assumed my connection to Havard and Arnbjorg was through multiple generations, and—wait. If Havard was my great-grandfather, didn't that make Yngvarr my great-uncle?

I blinked at him and sorta sensed my mouth was hanging open, so he gave me a strange look like I was obviously having a stroke in the middle of a swampy street in this Houstonian Hell. I thought Keira was asking me, repeatedly, what was wrong, but I was staring at my *great-uncle*, so I could only groan and rub my temples and curse Havard for not telling me just how closely related we actually were.

When my friends began to threaten to carry me out of Dante's Hell, despite how far we'd come in saving this city, I finally mumbled, "Headache. Just give me a minute." And I was only kinda lying, because thinking about my relationship to a god I considered a good friend now and to one who was hanging out inside my head or in my genes or something who just happened to be my great-grandfather really *was* giving me a headache. But the biggest, most tangible part of this revelation was that Yngvarr *looked* my age, and *oh holy Hell, my great-uncle and I had slept with the same goddess.*

I groaned again and squatted toward the street despite the stench rising from the brownish green algae covering the asphalt. Havard sighed loudly in my head and snapped, "*You're focusing on the wrong information here, dumbass.*"

So aloud, I snapped back, "*You're* the dumbass."

Agnes put her hand on one hip and raised an eyebrow at me as she stared down at me. "I'm going to assume that wasn't directed at one of us."

I shook my head, but slowly since Havard really had given me a migraine.

"I'm also going to assume this sudden headache is the result of a memory that's not good news."

Why did Agnes have to be so damn smart?

"It's... shocking news," I managed to say. "Give me a moment to process."

They shuffled their feet but waited patiently and silently for me to process the unprocessable. And yes, I know that's not a word, but *you* try discovering the dead god living inside your genes and directing you through a potentially catastrophic supernatural war is your great-grandfather.

Havard sighed loudly again, and I could almost feel him tapping his foot and drumming his fingers as he waited for me to get to the whole point of his memory. And go figure: he was right again. I *was* focusing on all the wrong parts of his story.

Because I'd somehow completely overlooked that my mother was his granddaughter, that he'd specifically told Áki to make sure she one day received the Sword of Asgard so she could hand it over to me when the time came.

Which meant my mother had had the Sword of Asgard all along.

"Oh, my God," I whispered.

Keira crouched beside me and touched my arm and said, "Gavyn, you're scaring me. What's wrong?"

But I couldn't tell her. Not here where we had to assume all of our conversations could be overheard by the gods who were trying to kill us, by the gods who wanted *my* sword, the one my mom had likely planned to give me as soon as Ninurta showed up and it became obvious this was the moment her father had warned her about. But cancer had robbed her of that chance.

By the time she knew she wouldn't be defeating this gods-awful disease, she probably didn't have the presence of mind to realize she should have told me, even though I was only twelve, that she had something hidden for me somewhere. Or maybe she thought it would be more dangerous to tell me too soon and too young, that I wouldn't believe her about its significance and would end up doing something really stupid, like one day bragging to my friends about the cool Viking sword my mom had inherited and left me, which would've made me an easy target for Odin.

Yeah, that was probably it.

I sensed Havard squirming a bit like he was suddenly nervous, but when he finally spoke to me again, I understood why. Thinking about my mom wasn't easy for him either. And because I hadn't been shocked enough for one day, I discovered he'd actually *known* her.

My mom had been born in Asgard.

"*You know where it is*," I said. "*You know where my mom hid our sword.*"

"*Not exactly. But I have a pretty good idea how we can track it down.*"

I exhaled heavily and stood up, aggravated and frustrated that he'd allow me to go through a literal *hell* when he could have directed me to this damn sword already and we could have ended this nightmare for everyone.

"*Gavyn, it's not that simple. Possessing the sword too soon would have meant risking it falling into the hands of our enemies. You have to trust me.*"

"*Cut the shit, Havard! If Mom was going to give it to me as soon as Ninurta and his gang started threatening the world—*"

But he interrupted me as he tried to explain, again, why he obviously thought I was the most incompetent dumbass in the world. "*She never planned to keep the sword in Asgard. She knew the whole story, what happened to her grandmother and me, and why Odin wanted this sword so badly. When she got sick, she had no choice but to bring it home.*"

"And?" I snapped, realizing a bit too late I'd forgotten to keep my end of the conversation silent.

But Havard didn't get the chance to explain why it mattered whether the sword was in Asgard or on Earth or how he sorta knew where it was but "not exactly," because a thick fog rolled over the marshy landscape, and if there was one thing I'd learned from countless horror movies over the years, it was that fog never concealed anything good.

"This had better not be nerve gas again," Agnes mumbled.

I nodded even though she was still watching the fog roll toward us, tumbling in on itself like it was being carried forward by a tornado. "I've got a long list of mutants that had better not be inside, too, starting with those devil dogs."

I thought I saw her cringe, but she put her warrior face back on so quickly, I might've just imagined it.

Ra tilted his face toward the dull sky and sighed loudly. "This world isn't real so I can't force the sun's heat to burn away this fog."

"Feels pretty real to me," I complained.

"It's real enough," a voice from the fog responded. Now normally, I would've freaked the hell out about talking fog, but after discovering the dead god who'd taken up residence in my head months ago was my great-grandfather and my mother wasn't even born in this world and had probably *grown up* in some alternate universe, I doubted much would ever really freak me the hell out again.

Except devil dogs. Those bastards would always scare the shit out of me.

A man's figure emerged from the fog that had gotten close enough to us that I could smell the rotten stench of the marsh combined with something acrid, something unique to this whitish-gray cloud of putridness.

The man emerged from the ammonia-riddled mist, and I was admittedly a *little* surprised that he looked pretty normal. I mean, he was wearing a tattered and stained chiton, which I guessed wasn't really *normal*, but he was just a guy with short brown hair and dark eyes and a closely cropped beard. His leather sandals looked like they'd seen better days, so my stupid traitorous mouth decided to do what it did best and start talking without my permission. "Does the Fifth Circle of Hell have a homelessness problem?"

And, of course, my great-uncle, being too closely related to me, immediately answered, "It's *Hell*. I'm pretty sure everyone's homeless and *everything* is a problem."

The homeless guy looked over his shoulder where the fog was clearing, revealing the slimy marsh with the same people attempting to cross its surface and slipping and reaching for a shore they'd never touch. "I'm here to ferry you across. If you want to get to the Sixth Circle, you'll have to ride with me."

I snorted and shook my head, so he shot me a curious look. "No way are we going anywhere with you."

"And why would you help us?" Keira demanded.

"I'm not," the man said. "Do you think it's helpful to reach farther into the depths of Hell?"

Agnes was squinting at the guy like she sorta recognized him but couldn't quite remember him, like she'd met him at some office party where she'd gotten totally hammered and was just hoping she hadn't woken up beside him. And if she *had*, I'd put money on this guy doing it with the eighteen-thousand-year-old witch because he struck me as a total perv who'd do someone like that.

"Phlegyas," she finally said.

The man nodded in acknowledgment.

So, naturally, I leaned over and loudly whispered, "Did you sleep with him or something?"

"Gavyn," Keira groaned.

And Phlegyas just looked Agnes over and said, "Pretty sure I'd remember *her*."

"I'm going to kill him," Agnes announced.

"I think he's already dead," Yngvarr said.

"Then I'll kill him again," Agnes insisted.

So Yngvarr just shrugged and agreed that sounded like a good plan and totally possible.

Phlegyas rubbed his eyes and grunted, and I'm not gonna lie: I kinda liked that we had the ability to annoy the hell out of some dead guy who haunted swamps and tried to lure unsuspecting visitors into his creepy pervert van. Okay, he *technically* had a boat, but it was still a creepy pervert boat.

"Look," Phlegyas said. "This is all part of my eternal damnation. I'm just supposed to ferry you across the marsh and bring you to the next circle. If you don't want to go, then stay here. I honestly don't care about your fates."

I again leaned closer to Agnes and loudly whispered, "Dante's *Inferno* is fiction, right? So who the hell *are* all these people and monsters we've been fighting?"

"These gods and spirits are real," Agnes explained. "But this entire city is under a powerful curse, and it's forced them to believe they're actually in the different circles of Hell."

I pretended to think about that, mostly just because it seemed to make me smarter than I actually was, and nodded. "Does anyone remember if this guy is legit or not?"

"Legit," Ra repeated. "As in legitimately a ghost?"

"No, legitimately just offering to bring us across the swamp, no strings attached," I explained.

Ra shrugged and stepped toward the dead Greek guy, grabbing his arm and yanking him closer to our group of tired heroes and gods who all desperately needed showers. "Feels real enough. If he's lying to us, we'll just throw him out the boat and take ourselves across."

I gaped at the sun god because it seemed like a remarkably simple plan to just steal the guy's boat and ferry ourselves across anyway. But Phlegyas shook his head and told us, "You won't be able to cross without me. Go ahead and try, but you'll encounter the same problem as all those condemned to walk this marsh. The closer you think you're getting to the other side, the farther it will actually become."

"Son of a bitch," I sighed.

"All right," Keira said. "Take us across. But if you're lying—"

"Why would I lie?" he asked, but he sounded completely fed up and weary already. And we hadn't even *begun* our trip across the marsh. "Believe me: I want to be rid of you all as soon as possible."

"That I actually believe," I agreed.

So we all climbed into the dead Greek pervert's boat, although we made him stand as far away from us as possible, which wasn't nearly far enough considering there was just enough room for the six of us. He stuck a long pole into the murky water and pushed us away from the bank, watching the opposite shoreline like it was bringing him to the Promised Land, which it sort of was since that's where he'd finally be able to get away from us once and for all.

We were halfway across the swamp when I caught myself staring at Yngvarr again, who was staring back at me like I was having another stroke, and heard myself blurt out, "You knew my mom."

This seemed to startle not only Yngvarr, but Keira and Agnes as well. And while Ra seemed interested in that "this could be a good story" kind of way, he didn't quite understand the significance of my unexpected announcement.

"Okay," Yngvarr said slowly. "Did I know her well?"

I glanced at Phlegyas, but he was still hyper-focused on the shore and getting us there as quickly as possible. "Maybe. At least when she was little. I'm not sure how long you knew her."

"Is she..." he began, but he didn't seem to know how to ask how closely related they were. And since he'd heard every story thus far, and undoubtedly remembered every detail, I decided to tell him in the most innocuous way possible.

"She's Astrid's daughter." I took a deep breath and turned my attention toward Keira. "And Áki's."

Her eyes widened, but they all understood the dangers of saying too much. Revealing just that information had probably been too much, but since Havard hadn't piped in to tell me to keep my dumb mouth shut yet, I figured our fairly cryptic conversation was okay.

Yngvarr and Keira both lowered their heads and stared

blankly at the bottom of the boat, lost in the same kind of shock I'd succumbed to fifteen minutes ago when Havard body-slammed me with this memory. It was Agnes who reached over my great-uncle and took my hand, and in her always brilliant way, found words to reassure me without giving anything away to our enemies who were almost certainly eavesdropping somehow. "There is something comforting in the discovery of family, in understanding where we've come from. I've always found it helps us make sense of our own lives."

I smiled weakly at her, no longer nearly as unsettled by her moments of compassion as I used to be, but Phlegyas stood up straighter and lifted his pole from the water. Moments later, the boat gently rocked onto a muddy bank and he beckoned us to stand and disembark. But as Ra, the last of us to step onto the land marking the Sixth Circle, joined us, Phlegyas's smile turned sinister and his parting words sounded like a eulogy rather than a casual farewell.

"And it came to pass when the children of men had multiplied that in those days were born unto them beautiful and comely daughters. And the angels, the children of the heaven, saw and lusted after them, and said to one another: 'Come, let us choose wives from among the children of men and beget us children.' And Semjâzâ, who was their leader, said unto them: 'I fear ye will not indeed agree to do this deed, and I alone shall have to pay the penalty of a great sin.' And they all answered him and said: 'Let us all swear an oath, and all bind ourselves by mutual imprecations not to abandon this plan but to do this thing.' Then swear they all together and bound themselves by mutual imprecations upon it. And they were in all two hundred, who descended in the days of Jared on the summit of Mount Hermon."

While my allies fell silent, seemingly terrified by this strange diatribe of a dead Greek asshole, I threw my hands up and exclaimed, "And what the hell is *that* supposed to mean?"

But it was Agnes who answered me. "It means," she said quietly, "that guarding those walls around the Sixth Circle are two hundred fallen angels."

CHAPTER EIGHT

Thinking about having to fight my way through *two hundred* fallen angels made my skin break out in a cold sweat, and I actually started shivering despite the overwhelming heat of this part of Hell. Even Havard was sweating —metaphorically, of course, since he no longer had a body— which didn't bode well for the rest of us.

"Now I know why that prick was so eager to get us across the swamp," I complained.

Agnes nodded and warily eyed the massive walls in front of us. So far, no sign of any angels: fallen or not, although I wasn't really sure we'd have to worry about any not-fallen angels. Just beyond the walls, flames leapt into the blood-red sky, and Keira inched a bit closer to me and slipped her hand inside of mine. I pretended it was because she needed my comfort, but truthfully, this was, by far, the most terrifying of the circles we'd yet to encounter and I kinda felt better with her so close.

"So how did you know what Phlegm was talking about?" I asked Agnes.

"Phlegyas," she corrected. "And because he was quoting the *Book of Enoch*."

I would have asked her what *that* was, but truthfully, I didn't care. I was staring at a huge wall with fires raging behind it and waiting for a couple hundred fallen angels to charge us and kick our asses. "So," I said. "Who's going first?"

Ra glanced in my direction and replied, "You're the hero. Pretty sure this is one of those moments where you're supposed to prove your heroism."

"I don't need to," I retorted. "Everyone already knows I'm really a coward who just gets lucky sometimes. Besides, if there were ever a time for a witch to—"

"Gavyn," Agnes warned, so I grinned at her and decided to lay off the witch accusations until we were out of Dante's Hell because she looked like *she* was ready to kick my ass, even without the help of two hundred fallen angels.

"One final question," I said instead. "Was I understanding Phlegm—"

"Phlegyas," Agnes and Keira interrupted.

I ignored them both. "Correctly when he was babbling that these angels all got kicked out of Heaven for doing it with women?"

"Yes," Agnes answered.

So I figured I *really* needed to confirm this because only guys, even angelic guys, would be that stupid. "They fell because they were horny."

"Yes," Agnes answered again.

I nodded and pretended like that was a perfectly good reason to get booted from Heaven. "I *have* done some pretty stupid shit just because I wanted to get laid."

"No kidding," Keira mumbled.

I couldn't quite tell if I actually blushed a bit or if my skin was just melting off my face since it was at *least* seven thousand degrees in the Sixth Circle, but either way, I decided it was a good time to hunt down those horny angels.

As we neared the wall, which seemed to grow taller the closer we got and not just in that visual perspective kind of way, Yngvarr pointed out the obvious. "Is there a gate? We're not supposed to climb over this thing, are we?"

And that was apparently the cue the angels were waiting for.

Forms materialized all around us, and okay, I totally expected robed guys with feathery wings, but instead, we'd been surrounded by tall, shimmering figures, as if their entire bodies were made of some sort of blue fire. We pressed closer to one another as the angels closed in on us and Ra murmured, "Any chance you know the *Book of Enoch* well enough that you can tell us how these fallen angels were defeated?"

"Yeah," Agnes said. "God sent a flood."

"Wait," I interjected, "*the* flood? Like Noah's ark flood?" Because, clearly, that was the most important conversation for us to have at the moment.

"Yes," Agnes snapped. "Not only were there a bunch of asshole angels, but a bunch of asshole Nephilim and men were slaughtering each other because *these* particular assholes taught them warfare, okay?"

These particular assholes—the blue-fire angels—paused as if surprised by Agnes's outburst and her willingness to so openly insult them when we were outnumbered, and let's face it, overpowered. Sure, three of us were gods but I had yet to figure out what great advantage *that* conferred considering I'd fought quite a few gods and they fought back with swords and spears just like any mortal.

Wait: just like any mortal from the *Middle Ages,* I mean.

"Please tell me one of you has the ability to make it rain then," I murmured.

"Two war gods and a sun god," Keira sighed. "We should've chosen our companions better."

"Judas," Agnes said.

"So none of us can make it rain," Yngvarr pointed out. "We need another option."

And, really, when surrounded by glowing, angry celestial—or formerly celestial?—creatures, there was only one thing I *could* do. "Okay, guys, let's talk," I shouted at them. "I'm willing to bet you're all angry that you jumped ship to hook up with a bunch of women, and I'm with you. That whole 'no sex' rule is totally bogus. And after getting kicked out of Heaven and everything, you end up *here*. This is a raw deal."

"Gavyn," Keira hissed. "*What* are you doing?"

I shrugged and whispered back, "Hell if I know." But the fallen angels, who held what appeared to be flaming blue swords but since they were identical to their flaming blue bodies, maybe they all just had one really weird arm, had stopped their advance. I had the feeling they were gaping at me, or at the very least, staring at me and wondering the same thing as Keira: what *was* I doing?

"Look," I continued, because I couldn't figure out a different way to buy us time other than talking, "it seems like shit gets real beyond those walls and there's a significant chance none of us are going to make it out of there alive, so you might as well let us pass and one of the asshole monsters in there can take care of us. We don't—"

The fallen angels made an odd, hair-raising sound that might have been laughter or a summons to the Devil himself, where honestly, I drew the line. I mean, another line. So I had a lot of lines.

"I don't think asking nicely worked," Agnes said. "I do, however, think you managed to piss them off... not that any of us are surprised by that."

So I retorted, "It's not like I have a brothel I can distract them with." And go figure, the fallen angels didn't seem to like my implication they could be easily distracted by the promise of sex. I only knew they were insulted by the intensity of those flames glowing brighter, and I silently cursed myself and told Havard, "*All right, wake your lazy ass up and help us here.*"

And all I got in return was, "*Um...*"

"Screw it," I muttered. I raised my sword and advanced on the nearest flaming blue dude, who seemed surprised by my sudden moxie, which is probably the only reason I didn't die. His fiery blue sword caught the edge of mine before I could slice off the angel's arm—wait... I don't feel comfortable saying I was trying to kill an angel even if it was a fallen angel, so I'll call them demons from now on—and the bastard parried and almost chopped off my head.

Given these *demons* were like ten feet tall, they already had a significant advantage, which meant we likely couldn't beat them in a swordfight, and we needed a different strategy. I glanced behind the demon, who was *definitely* pissed off now, toward the angry, raging fires consuming all those tortured souls. I had another most likely idiotic idea, and if it *did* turn out to be completely disastrous, I was blaming it on Havard. I mean, how would anyone know it wasn't his idea?

"Ra," I yelled as I blocked another attempt at my decapitation. "Can you spread those fires?"

My allies were busy trying to keep their own heads attached to their bodies, but Ra called back, "To where?"

"Here," I shouted. "If we can't drown these bastards, let's burn them!"

Now, sure these demons already appeared to be on fire, but it was a totally different kind of fire, so immolating them with *regular* fire could work... right?

Havard finally spoke up to tell me, "*Immolate implies there's a sacrifice being made, so to whom exactly are you sacrificing these fallen angels?"*

That was how he decided to help me? What was the point of having a dead great-grandfather semi-reincarnated in my genes if *that* was his idea of helping out? I sighed heavily, ducked beneath the bright blue sword swinging toward my neck and wished, for the millionth time, Havard still had an ass so I could kick it.

But the conversation between Ra and me about spreading those fires *did* make many of the demons pause again. Of course, it also made my friends pause to give me the all too familiar, "*Why* are you such a dumbass?" look, but Ra humored me anyway. The fires inside the walls leapt over those massive fortifications and raced across the ground, crackling and sizzling as they devoured everything in their path.

I realized a moment too late that *we* were also in their path, but the demons lowered their swords as the flames licked their feet. For a heart-pounding second, the only sound outside the Sixth Circle of Hell was the ferocious crackling and spitting of that fire, but the demons broke the silence by unleashing this unholy scream that would have shattered glass if there had been any within a twenty-mile radius. The fire crept up their bodies as they writhed and protested with that shrieking that I was pretty sure would permanently deafen me, but they clearly weren't immune to fire.

Of course, neither were we, but Ra somehow kept the small circle of ground where we stood free of those deadly flames. As they reached the fallen angels' heads, the screaming stopped and all around us, those flickering blue figures broke apart, sending a sparkling blue mist into the otherwise gray sky.

When we were sure no more demons were lurking beyond the flames, Ra extinguished his fire, leaving only ash on the equally gray ground. Somehow, even the swampy areas outside those walls had burned and only thin vapors remained.

And in what should have been a warning to us all, a gate appeared in the wall, open and unguarded. But we'd come this far, and if Anhur held the key to finding Ninurta and Inanna, we had no choice but to enter the final Gates of Hell.

THREE CIRCLES lay side by side like a circus, only this one was more like pain and misery than fun and whimsy. As soon as Yngvarr, the last of us to enter, stepped inside the walls, the gate slammed shut then disappeared altogether.

I blinked stupidly at the now solid wall and smartly observed, "That doesn't seem ominous at all."

"Neither do the centaurs galloping around that river of blood," Agnes added, nodding toward what actually *were* centaurs on patrol around a river of blood.

Ra wrinkled his nose and jutted his chin toward the second ring. "Nor do a bunch of thorny trees and bushes filled with harpies."

One of the harpies shrieked at us as if agreeing their presence wasn't ominous for our fates at all.

Keira folded her arms over her chest and scowled at the third circle. "I am *not* going through there."

The sand dunes seemed harmless enough, but the fiery rain immediately nixed any plans to attempt traversing that circle. And given Odin's supreme evilness, we could *hear* people screaming in all three rings, but we couldn't see them. And maybe it was slightly better for me, anyway, since my overbearing demigod genes were already itching to go into each circle and rescue whomever was screaming like that. If I'd been able to see them, I probably wouldn't have been able to stop myself and would've died right there in the Three Ring Circus of Horrors.

"We'll have to go between the circles," Agnes said quietly. "The centaurs are patrolling between one and two, so our best shot will be between two and three."

"All that means is that we'll get attacked by some mystery monster instead of horse men," I countered.

"Undoubtedly," she said, but she actually walked away from me, heading toward the narrow space between the second and third circles. And, of course, Yngvarr immediately followed her, the dumb lovesick idiot. But then Havard's obnoxiously domineering genes took over, and I found *my* dumb overprotective ass following my great-uncle. And calling him that *still* made me cringe and silently curse my great-grandfather, who'd gone back to ignoring me, not that he'd been useful at all lately.

Keira kept pace with me and would occasionally steal glances in my direction, so I finally slowed down to buy us a little privacy. "Why are you acting like I'm going to drop dead any second?" I asked. But then I thought about my prophecy and added, "*Am* I going to drop dead at any second?"

Keira shook her head and whispered, "Havard shared something with you earlier... something huge. I just need to know if... I mean, Áki. Do you...?"

I started to tell her that I'd share everything as soon as we were out of Odin's Hell, but in a way, discovering my ancestry *did* have a significant impact on her as well, and of course she'd want to know all about my grandfather. And that was exactly what she was trying to ask me: if I'd ever known her adopted son.

Now here's the thing: I'd *met* both of my maternal grandparents. Actually, they were still alive, and lived in upstate New York, so I didn't see them that often, but I *knew* them. And they weren't named Áki and Astrid but Paul and Clara. I found myself thinking maybe I really *was* just going crazy and none of these conversations with Havard or reliving his memories or even the dreams were real.

"If I were losing my mind and imagining all of this, even the battles and being here, I wouldn't really know it, would I?" I whispered back. "Crazy people don't know they're crazy, right?"

"You're not crazy, Gavyn," Keira tried to assure me, but if *she* were just a hallucination, I'd expect her to say that.

Agnes glanced over her shoulder and scolded us. "Hurry up, you two. If you think hanging back will get you out of fighting whatever's ahead—"

"Just use your witch powers," I snapped back, forgetting I'd vowed to lay off the witchy accusations until we were out of Houston. "I'm tired of doing all the grunt work."

Agnes made an entirely inappropriate gesture in response then faced forward again, but we'd almost reached the narrow passageway between the second and third rings, and I didn't know *what* to tell Keira so I just landed on the truth. I leaned as close as I could while still walking and whispered, "According to Havard, Áki is my grandfather, only he goes by Paul now and lives outside of Syracuse."

Keira was so surprised that she stumbled, and I had to grab her arm to keep her from falling. She turned her beautiful blue eyes toward me and I could *see* the thousand unspoken questions, but we'd reached the passageway and something was already moving in the shadows, emitting an odd snuffling sound that made me suspect we were about to encounter some sort of animal rather than a god or another fallen angel.

Turns out, I was only sorta right, because what burst out of the alley between the circles was every bit as horrifying as those damn devil dogs. With some nightmarish cross between a dragon and a scorpion, this bastard had a *human face*, and just like those hellhounds I despised so much, he hissed my name, too. And *only* my name.

"Are you *kidding* me?" I shouted-complained at the deformed dragon.

"Gavyn," he hissed angrily.

"Geryon," Ra said.

"No," I corrected. "My name really is Gavyn. He's saying it correctly."

Ra's mouth fell open, but I'd apparently rendered him speechless. Agnes was the one who had to tell me I was still the reigning monarch of Idiot Village. "The *dragon* is Geryon." She gave Keira a puzzled look and jerked her thumb toward me. "Seriously? *This* is the guy you fall for?"

I half expected Keira to defend me, but she just shrugged and said, "I think Fate has a cruel sense of humor."

And Geryon added, "Gavyn."

"Okay," I said, "one devil dragon shouldn't be *that* hard." I braced myself for the impending fight, but it was like we were back in Sumer II where even our thoughts made all sorts of evil shit materialize, all of which tried to kill us. Behind Geryon, a dozen more identical dragon men appeared, *all* hissing my name.

I took a step back, then another one, then turned around to run, but Keira grabbed the back of my shirt and refused to let me take off.

Yngvarr and Agnes sheathed their swords, which may have led to a smattering of profane curses from me, but Yngvarr shouted, "You wanted to know what war gods could do, right?"

"Die like a couple of dumbasses?" I shouted back.

The dragon men had almost reached our small group, and my heart sank. I couldn't actually watch my friends die. I tried to break free from Keira's grasp, but she refused to let go of my shirt still, and I couldn't wriggle out of it without dropping my shield and sword. And I wasn't dying weaponless like the two dumbasses at the fore of our group.

But Agnes and Yngvarr stood perfectly still, unconcerned about the mutant dragon men about to attack them. And that was probably because the mutant dragon men never *did* attack them. Instead, Geryon, who led the mutant army, suddenly turned on his fellow bastardized dragon creatures and attacked *them*. In fact, they all began to fight one another, ripping at each other's bodies with their long claws and biting at the throats of their brethren, which reminded me of the damn vampires back in Baton Rouge and Thor who was still in the hospital and just how tired I was of having to combat all these monsters and gods.

"Wait," I said. "You have the power to turn our enemies against each other, and you're just now using it?"

I was seriously tempted to hit them both with my shield, worm out of Keira's grasp, and return to the real world forever... maybe even head to Syracuse and move in with my apparently semi-godly grandmother who'd obviously been lying to me my whole life. But honestly, that *still* seemed like a better option than staying with the gods who'd been lying to me for months.

At least my grandmother had never tried to kill me.

But Yngvarr quickly explained, "We can't *always* influence our enemies. It doesn't work on gods because their power is as great as our own. And when you were in Sumer II with Agnes, *everyone's* powers were diminished. Odin's curse on Houston is powerful, but it's also spread out, much more so than the one in Baton Rouge, so his magic is spread thin in places."

"And since this is one of those places, it may be that he knew what lies ahead is a greater threat than Geryon's battalion," Agnes added.

"Still seems like this is a power you could have used long before now," I muttered.

Agnes shrugged and said, "I have. Doesn't mean we can always get out of fighting though. Sometimes, it just makes our battles a little easier."

The last pair of dragon men that were ripping each other apart finally fell to the ground, bloodied and twitching, but their bodies stilled and Yngvarr waved us forward. "We're getting close," he said, stepping over the body of a shredded dragon with a man's face. "Only two more circles of Hell exist, and we know Anhur won't be alone. We'll have no choice but to fight our way through the last circle."

Ra's expression hardened and he said, "But Anhur must survive long enough for me to find out how we can reach Ninurta and Inanna, or we've wasted all this time and effort."

"And after you get that information from him?" I asked. "What then?"

Ra's already dark eyes seemed to darken further and in a chillingly flat voice, he answered, "And then I'm going to kill him."

CHAPTER NINE

Passing into the Eighth Circle was a lot like going back in time to that pit where Plutus had brutally imprisoned all those innocent people with heavy stones tied around their necks. Only this circle contained even deeper trenches with sharper rocks and demons—not fallen angels, which were admittedly beautiful but terrifying at the same time—but actual grappling-hook clawed demons who looked ready to rip my skin from my body.

It goes without saying—of course, I'm going to say it anyway—that I thought that was also a completely unacceptable way to die.

As we wove our way between the trenches, trying to avoid peering into them so we wouldn't see the sources of all that screaming and wailing, large shadows began to emerge from the edges of the ring. Whatever was approaching us had been hiding by the wall that encircled the trenches, and Keira and I slowed down to get a better look at those dark shapes. We were both obviously having a hard time convincing our brains that what our eyes thought they were seeing was real.

"Are those..." she stammered, "dinosaurs?"

"Um…" I answered.

The gods stopped, too, seemingly as confused as Keira and me. "That is definitely a large reptile of some sort," Yngvarr agreed.

"Komodo dragon on steroids?" I guessed.

A pained, gut-wrenching wail on our opposite side turned our attention away from the dinosaur impersonators to a group of ambling humans milling around the wall of the Eighth Circle. I squinted at them and said, "Flaming zombie monkeys are one thing. But zombie humans are definitely a deal breaker."

"Don't worry," Agnes assured me. "Zombies go after brains, so you're safe."

I flipped her off before agreeing with her.

But Ra stepped a bit closer to the crowd and shook his head. "Not zombies. Those people are sick."

"Clearly, you've never seen *The Walking Dead*," I countered. "Being sick is how it starts."

But Ra stubbornly insisted those people were not infected with some mystery zombie virus, but a very real and very frightening bacteria that would likely kill many of the infected people if we didn't hurry.

"No," he said. "I've seen this before. Notice those dark, swollen nodes on their bodies? Those are buboes. These people have the plague."

"Plague," I repeated flatly. "As in *the* plague? The same one that wiped out half of Europe?"

Ra nodded, and my European allies stepped away from the diseased mob who'd noticed us now. Many of them were reaching toward us as if begging for relief or maybe to be put out of their misery.

Yngvarr urged us to keep going by quietly telling me, "I remember the Black Death. We need to get out of here."

Havard, who'd been pretty quiet lately, piped up to agree

with his brother. "*We can't help them except by lifting the curse. I'm pretty sure Odin didn't leave antibiotics lying around.*"

Even though I knew they were right, I had a hard time convincing my legs to start moving again. Intellectually—stop laughing, I can have intellectual thoughts—I understood the only way I could help these miserable humans was to end this curse, which *should* lift the afflictions all these Houstonians were suffering from, but at the same time, I felt like walking away now was essentially abandoning them to a fate worse than any I could imagine.

Some of the sicker people lying on the ground occasionally vomited blood, and even their noses, and hell, their *skin*, bled as the bacteria ravaged their bodies. How could we just walk away?

"It's septicemic," Keira told me. "We *have* to get to Anhur, Gavyn. There's no other way to save them, even if we *did* have access to doctors and medications."

"Isn't there—" I started to argue, but she cut me off by grabbing my hand and pulling me away from the diseased population of the Eighth Circle.

For a long time, none of us spoke, but I noticed Ra's face had taken on that steely, murderous expression again. The wall marking the entrance to the ninth and final circle of Hell loomed closer, so I finally got Ra's attention and reminded him, "We need to find out about Ninurta and Inanna first. You can't just kill Anhur as soon as we find him."

Ra didn't even acknowledge me at first, which only reinforced that whole Most Loathsome God in the Universe label, but just before passing through the gate, he gripped my arm and begged me, "If I look like I'm about to lose it, stop me, Gavyn. Only you *can*."

I blinked at him like this was some joke I didn't get, which actually seemed a hell of a lot more probable than my ability to stop a god on a murderous rampage without killing him. Because the only time I'd encountered gods on murderous rampages, that *was* the only way I could stop them. And I was still convinced most of the time, I'd just gotten extraordinarily lucky.

When Ra didn't offer a punch line, I sighed and asked, "Okay, how?"

He lifted a shoulder and replied, "You'll figure something out. You always do."

Then that bastard actually let go of my arm and passed through the gate into the Ninth Circle.

I lifted an eyebrow at Agnes who also just shrugged and followed Ra. Yngvarr didn't even give me a chance to shoot him my "What the bloody hell?" look before he disappeared through the gate as well, leaving me alone with Keira.

"Okay, one," I said, "I miss Hunter."

She stared blankly at me for a few moments then said, "Irrelevant. And two?"

"How am I supposed to stop Ra without killing him?"

Keira took a deep breath and ran her fingers through her long, blond hair. "There's something remarkable about the combination of genes between a god and a human. Heroes see the world differently than either race, and that confers special advantages on us. It's one of the reasons the gods need us."

I snorted and my mouth betrayed me for the millionth time. "Yeah, like enslaving us for eternity just to fill their warrior coffers?"

I immediately started to apologize, but Keira nodded and said, "The worst gods will do stuff like that. And how many times do we have to tell you not to use unusual words like 'coffers'?"

"I could know unusual words," I pouted.

Agnes poked her head through the gate and scolded, "Come on, you two. We're waiting and if you think you're getting out of venturing into the literal heart of Hell, I *will* turn you both into frogs."

I folded my arms and snapped, "I thought you weren't a witch."

"Let's not find out," Keira said.

She took a step closer to the gate, but before she could go further, I grabbed her arm and gently turned her toward me, kissing her quickly before just as quickly letting go and saying, "If we don't survive, I just needed you to know that I love you, that if I weren't fated to die anyway, I would've wanted to spend the rest of my life with you, even though you deserve someone so much better than me."

"Gavyn," she whispered, but I let go of her arm and stepped into the Ninth Circle of Hell where we would either *finally* discover how to reach the Sumerians responsible for starting this war, or our lives would end in sacrifices that came far too soon.

SO I KINDA EXPECTED the center of Hell to be hot... like fire and brimstone and skin melting off my bones kinda hot. What I *found,* though, was a frozen lake with four concentric circles, and throughout each lake, random heads popped out of the ice like they'd just been stuck there as macabre ornaments. But there was something strange about this final circle of Hell, something I strongly suspected wasn't in Dante Alighieri's original poem.

The Marriot where Hunter and I had once stayed when we saw the Astros play stood undisturbed behind the frozen circles. I mean, it's not like Anhur would want to give up his luxurious accommodations as the rest of Houston was thrust into agony and perpetual torment.

Asshole.

Ra's fingers had already curled into fists and his eyes blazed like the sun itself. Even from a distance, I could see the demigods patrolling the entrance to the hotel, and I counted twenty-three of them.

"Aren't you one of the most important gods in your pantheon?" I asked Ra.

Apparently, he'd lost his ability to speak because he just nodded, keeping his eyes fixed on the hotel.

"Think those demigods will listen to you then?" I pressed.

When he didn't answer, Yngvarr tried to help him out. "Not necessarily. After all, you didn't want to listen to Odin or, really, any of us."

"True," I acknowledged. "But I eventually mostly listened to Tyr, and—"

My throat clenched and refused to let me talk about my dead friend anymore. By the expression on Yngvarr and Keira's faces, they didn't want to talk about it either.

"Well," I said as nonchalantly as possible, which was probably not nonchalant at all, "guess we should fight our way in now."

Agnes sighed beside me and added, "I know I'm a war goddess and all, but I'm getting *really* tired of having to fight my way into every single place lately."

"Maybe you can turn *them* into frogs," I suggested.

"Or maybe," Keira said, "we could just march over there and get this over with."

"Killjoy," Agnes and I muttered.

Halfway through the tundra of the Ninth Circle, I actually found myself missing the scorching heat from earlier circles. A frigid gust of wind would occasionally hit us, and I would scowl even harder at the bundled up demigods who I *swear* were just standing there all smug and warm and mocking us poor bastards who were turning into deity-sicles. Or half-deity-sicles.

I tilted my face toward the sky, which was surprisingly blue like a normal sky rather than the dull gray I'd grown accustomed to in Odin's version of Hell, and asked Ra, "Can you heat this place up with the sun?"

He shook his head but *still* didn't speak or look away from the hotel we were quickly approaching.

Once again, Yngvarr had to answer for him. "Odin's curse is most powerful here. I'm afraid none of our powers will work in this final circle."

I grunted and mumbled, "I *really* hope I get the chance to kill that bastard." As usual, I remembered too late that *this* particular bastard was Keira's father so I glanced at her to apologize, but she just glanced back at me and said, "I'll help you."

So okay, my Valkyrie was totally into patricide. That was good to know.

As we stepped onto what *should* have been the driveway in front of the hotel, the heroes barring the entrance finally moved away from the doors, shouting at us in a language I didn't understand, and one Havard obviously didn't speak either since he was just as lost.

But Ra knew what they were saying and shouted back at them, and while their expressions indicated they were surprised and more than a little frightened, they didn't back down. Agnes leaned closer to me and whispered, "Arabic. I know about eight words in that language, so I have no idea what they're saying, but I'm pretty sure Ra just identified himself, which is why they all look like they're ready to shit themselves."

"Not that ready," I whispered back. "None of them are putting down their swords."

Agnes nodded and asked Ra, "Are we fighting our way in or what?"

And Ra *finally* spoke to us. "Yes. Leave none of them alive."

Some strange croaking sound may or may not have crept out of my throat, but come on... if one of these demigods laid down his weapon to surrender, I was supposed to ignore that and kill him anyway?

Havard reminded me, *"This is why Ra asked you to stop him from making catastrophic decisions. Remember the stories I've told you when I couldn't control my rage either. He needs you to act as his conscience."*

So, naturally, I snapped back, "I'm not Jiminy Cricket, Havard."

Even the Egyptian heroes, who probably didn't *speak* English, shot me strange looks like they were about to fight a crazy person, and really, they probably were.

Agnes snorted and nudged me forward. "Come on, Jiminy. Let's get inside this hotel so we can get back to civilization before the whole world goes to shit."

I sighed but did this amazingly cool and intimidating twirl of my sword as I prepared to engage one of the Egyptian demigods... okay, fine. I *attempted* to do this amazingly cool and intimidating twirl of my sword but dropped the damn thing on the frozen ground and had to hurriedly scoop it up before he impaled me with his own sword.

I thought they all laughed at me, but they could have been laughing at anything, really. I mean, Ra had clearly established himself as the comedic genius of the bunch, so they were probably just laughing at him.

My blunder had, however, cost me those few precious seconds during which I might have been able to take on two heroes at once, and now, they were both practically on top of me. For the hundredth time, Odin's shield saved my life as I held it above me so I could retrieve my weapon. As their swords made contact with the enchanted wood, their bodies were thrown back into the side of the hotel, giving me enough time to leap to my feet and charge them. And this time, I held onto the grip of my sword tightly instead of trying to show off like the dumbass I was and would always be.

One of the heroes regained his balance a little too quickly and thrust his blade, which honestly sounds a little perverted, toward my sternum. I twisted on my left heel and avoided having my heart introduced to a thirty-inch piece of iron, but before he could retract his sword, I swung mine straight down, separating his hand from his arm.

For a split second, neither of us reacted. I just kinda stood there, staring at the bloody hand on the ground, and he did the exact same thing. Oddly enough, his buddy, the other demigod who'd initially attacked me, reacted first by screaming something unintelligible in my direction and raising his sword above his head like he was Conan the Barbarian or something.

Now, look: I don't expect any of you to ever find yourselves engaged in a swordfight with a demigod in the Ninth Circle of Hell, but if you *do*, don't be the kind of dumbass who lifts your sole weapon over your head, leaving your entire chest and face exposed so your enemy can thrust his sword at your exposed body and impale you.

Which, by the way, is exactly what I did.

Since One Arm Joe was still just standing there stupidly, I spun around and put *him* out of his misery before quickly assessing how many demigods my friends had gotten out of our way. Only a few remained, and it looked like they were in the process of surrendering. Swords clinked to the frozen ground and their hands slowly rose into the air, but since I hadn't learned Arabic in the past sixty seconds, I had no idea what they were telling Ra. Not that it mattered. He stalked toward them, that fire still burning in his eyes and Havard shouted, "*Gavyn, stop him!*"

I wanted to ask him how I was supposed to do that, but I didn't have time. If I didn't move *now*, Ra would kill the remaining demigods even though they were surrendering, and even I knew that was wrong.

And, really, I could only think of one way to prevent their needless deaths. I ran between Ra and the heroes who I assumed were begging for mercy, blocking Ra's path. He paused and blinked at me before ordering, "Get out of my way, Gavyn."

"No," I said firmly. "You *asked* me to do this, remember? And I've gotten to know you pretty well lately. If I let you kill these men, you'll regret it. You'll be consumed with guilt, and I really don't want to hear you bitching about it for the next few thousand years."

He blinked at me again before reminding me, "You're mortal. I don't think you'll live that long."

I shrugged and said, "You might visit Valhalla sometimes. You should, actually. We have killer beer there."

Agnes snuck behind me and grabbed one of the surrendering heroes, pushing him to the ground and tying his hands behind his back. I couldn't figure out *where* she'd gotten rope, but that was really at the bottom of my list of mysteries at the moment.

"Gavyn," Ra said coldly, "these *men* have sided with evil. They have no right to mercy."

"Maybe not," I agreed. "But I don't want to be allies with the kind of gods who would make that choice for whatever power is greater than all of us."

His eyes never dimmed, those flames burning so brightly, I feared he wasn't even really *seeing* me, only the enemies he was convinced he needed to kill in order to avenge all the suffering he'd recently witnessed. And part of me got that.

Part of me wanted revenge, too. But it couldn't come like this, not at this price.

He stepped toward me, and I reacted, just as I had what seemed like ages ago when I'd thrown Frey into a hotel wall and badly injured him. My body moved but my mind didn't seem connected to it at all. And, suddenly, Ra's sword was on the ground and his arms were pinned beside him as I stared into those fiery eyes and in a voice that didn't sound like my own, I told him, "We are going inside to find your son. I need you to snap out of it, Ra, because I can't do this without your help."

I wasn't even sure he recognized me. Maybe he thought I was one of the demigods who'd just tried to kill him, but somehow, he couldn't break free from my grasp, and he slowly stopped struggling against me. It felt like years passed before he really *saw* me, and his eyes began to dim, recognition replacing the hatred that had colored them before.

He glanced down at his immobile arms then back at me. "Gavyn," he said quietly. "What the hell's going on? You know I'm straight, right?"

I snorted and let go of him.

He looked past me, so I followed his gaze and noticed our friends had tied up the remaining demigods who'd surrendered. When I faced Ra again, understanding had replaced his confusion. He cleared his throat, suddenly embarrassed, and scooped his sword from the ground. "Sorry," he mumbled. "I just—"

"We're almost done here," I interrupted. "Let's go find Anhur and get out of Odin's Hell. I have a sword to find and a few gods left to kill."

Ra shot me an awkward smile and nod, and for the first time since meeting *any* of these gods, I almost felt sorry for them. Something about their nature occasionally made it impossible for them to control their own emotions, and given how many times I'd made incredibly stupid decisions when I *was* in control of my emotions, I couldn't imagine the lifetime of regrets I'd have if I were a god.

Although to be honest, it kinda explained a lot about Zeus's stories, even though that guy was still one hell of a prick.

Yngvarr yanked the lobby's door open, and a warm gust of air greeted us. I almost sighed happily, but wisely managed to keep it in, because it was one thing to do or say something stupid in front of my friends. But go figure: the lobby wasn't empty.

Because there was Anhur, waiting for us just beyond the doors.

CHAPTER TEN

Surrounding Anhur were a number of gods who looked uneasy about Ra's presence here. But the Egyptian sun god didn't seem to notice them. His attention was focused solely on his son. "What have you done?" Ra asked him.

Anhur flashed a toothy smile at his father and extended his arms as if the answer should have been obvious. "I have reclaimed what is rightly mine."

"Rightly yours?" Ra repeated. "You have no right to anything. Not four thousand years ago, and certainly not now."

Anhur snorted and crossed his arms, defiant and petulant just like a spoiled child. "Your compassion limits you. It has always been your greatest weakness."

This totally seemed like a family matter, but I couldn't help myself. I *had* to say something. "Hey, butthead, compassion is the *only* thing that can save this world, so lay off your old man."

Anhur lifted an eyebrow at me and snickered again. "I still think the Norse dragged the wrong guy into this fight.

There's no way *you* were intended to be this great hero who's supposed to stop us."

I nodded and agreed with him, which only seemed to confuse him.

Ra briefly turned his attention toward the other gods in the room and said, "If you return now, Ma'at may have mercy on you depending on your actions lately, and you'll be allowed to remain with us. If she decides you are guilty of unconscionable acts, Anubis will decide your fates."

The gods exchanged uneasy glances, but Anhur quickly addressed them in an attempt to keep his followers where they were. "My father is only trying to scare you. He is assuming he and his allies will win here, but they are outnumbered and *when* we defeat them, you won't have to worry about judgments from a goddess who has held our fates in her hands for far too long."

Personally, I thought there was *way* too much talking and not nearly enough fighting, so I held my sword up and challenged the god closest to me. "Your boss is convinced you'll win here. Why don't we find out?"

The smirk on the god's face irritated the hell out of me, so when he lunged and sliced, I angrily knocked his blade away with my shield and yelled, "Sloppy technique! How old *are* you?"

The god bared his teeth but didn't answer, preferring to advance again in another futile attempt to separate me from some body part. By now, the familiar sounds of battle had joined this annoyingly smug god and me, but if I looked away to judge how my friends were doing, I'd likely end up with a missing limb or gigantic gash that would quickly lead to me bleeding to death. And that didn't seem like a particularly pleasant experience, so I wisely kept my focus on my opponent.

He lunged again, but this time, I was ready for his attack

since he was apparently a one-trick pony. I cut a huge gash in his neck, and blood immediately soaked his collar and began spreading down his chest. He wouldn't be able to stand much longer, let alone fight, so I carefully backed away from him and waited until he fell before checking on my allies.

Some of the gods must've decided to take Ra up on his offer to allow Ma'at to judge their degree of guilt, because their hands had been bound and they sat by the wall, watching the fights unfold but mostly impassive about the outcomes. I had no idea who'd found the time to bind their hands amidst a huge swordfight, but far stranger things had happened in the last few months, so I decided not to worry about it.

What *didn't* surprise me was seeing Ra and Anhur engaged in battle, and even though Anhur was a war god, Ra was holding his own against him. But I was desperate to get out of this cursed city, so I crept behind them, pretending to stalk a particularly large god who was fleeing from Agnes. Once I was behind Anhur, I pivoted and jabbed the tip of my sword into the base of his skull, drawing blood but not enough to seriously injure him.

"Drop your sword," I ordered.

Anhur hesitated, but what could he really do? If he refused to comply, I could easily kill him. But he understood more of our motivations than I'd thought, and instead of dropping his sword, he laughed and said, "Go ahead, Gavyn. Kill me. It's already over, you know. You can't reach Ninurta, and by the time he returns, he'll be unstoppable... even for a *hero* like you."

I didn't like the way he said "hero" so I poked him a bit with the tip of my sword, drawing a few more drops of blood. Keira had joined me and folded her arms, scowling at the back of Anhur's head. "He's bluffing," she decided. "Even if

Ninurta returns with a larger army than we've yet seen, our allies have been amassing one, too."

Anhur laughed again, cutting off anything else Keira might've added to reassure us both that we *could* defeat this god who was responsible for completely uprooting my life. Sure, it hadn't been *much* of a life, waiting tables, sleeping around, drinking too much on more than a few occasions... okay, so maybe this hero gig wasn't *all* bad. Except for the whole fated to die part.

"Ninurta no longer needs an army," Anhur said.

I glanced over his shoulder toward Ra, hoping he'd explain what his son was talking about, and he didn't disappoint me. But, ultimately, I'd wished he hadn't known after all.

"The source of a god's power," he murmured.

"Dude," I snapped. "My arm is getting tired here. Either tell me straight up or let me impale this asshole."

"Believers," Keira offered. "The more believers a god has, the more powerful he is. But wouldn't *more* people be on our side? Shouldn't Agnes and Yngvarr and all of our allies be the ones getting far stronger?"

Ra shook his head but then totally contradicted himself, which just made me want to drop *my* sword and march over there to slap him. "Yes." He shook his head again and added, "I mean, no. It's not that simple anymore, because what I fear Ninurta is doing is convincing mortals to sacrifice themselves for his benefit."

"Um... *what?*" I asked.

"*Gavyn,*" Havard whispered in my mind. "*This could be...*" He paused and if a crazy voice in my head could take a deep breath, he was probably doing just that. "*If Anhur is telling the truth, we may not be able to stop him.*"

But since no one else could hear the conversation in my head, Ra told me, "Human sacrifices... they don't just surrender their bodies to the gods, Gavyn, but their souls."

"And what," I said. "A soul is like a supercharged battery?"

Agnes shrugged. "Something like that. It has the power to keep an existence going even after a body dies, so you do the math."

"I suck at math," I mumbled.

"We need to find Ninurta immediately," Ra announced, like that hadn't already become painfully obvious. But the bastard suddenly disappeared, leaving the rest of us to stare stupidly at the lobby floor where the sun god had been standing.

"*Told* you he was the Most Loathsome God in the Universe," I announced.

"I agree," Anhur said.

"*You* shut up," Keira snapped at Anhur then, to me, asked, "When did you tell us he was the Most Loathsome God in the Universe?"

"Oh," I said. "I guess I'd only told myself that."

Keira rolled her eyes, but the Most Loathsome God in the Universe returned, only he hadn't come back alone. Yet another beautiful goddess stood beside him, but unlike Isis, this one didn't seem to carry any disdain for this planet or the people on it. And Agnes obviously knew her, because she nodded respectfully and greeted her. "Ma'at. It's been a long time."

"It has," Ma'at agreed. "I wish we were meeting again under far better circumstances."

Agnes nodded again, and Ma'at squinted at Anhur as if already judging his degree of guilt.

But as usual, I was wrong. Ra hadn't brought her here to tell us what we already knew, but to discover what we otherwise couldn't.

"Brother," she said coldly, so naturally, I shot Keira my best "Huh?" look and she mouthed, "Ra's daughter."

If Ma'at knew what we were doing, and she probably did

considering we were standing right behind Anhur, she wisely ignored us. "Where is Ninurta?"

Anhur swallowed but refused to speak.

Ma'at stepped closer to him and repeated her question. "*Where* is Ninurta?"

"I..." he croaked but stubbornly clenched his jaw. I couldn't see his face clearly from this angle, but I imagined his eyes had taken on that wild, caged-animal look, because his sister obviously had some superpower to compel people to tell the truth.

Ma'at pulled the sword from his hand and tossed it aside then wrapped her fingers tightly around his arm, repeating her question for the third time. Anhur groaned, and I *swear* his skin seemed to glow a strange crimson color, like Ma'at would literally pull the truth from him if she had to.

I suddenly understood the fear all the Egyptian gods had displayed when Ra threatened to haul them off to his daughter, and how appealing the promise of her leniency must've been. And some of those dumbasses had still refused. Perhaps if they'd lived, they could've taken my King of the Village Idiots crown from me, but since we'd killed them all, I was still in no danger of losing my title.

Anhur grunted and in a quick, hissing breath, I *thought* the words, "Grande Terre," seeped out, but those were meaningless words to me. And not even English. But then I brightened up a bit and exclaimed, "Wait. He's in *Louisiana*? Still?"

"I don't think Anhur means *that* Grande Terre," Keira said. "Right?"

Ma'at tilted her head at her brother and her fingers tightened around his bicep, causing him to scream in pain, but I doubted it was from her grip. "Desolation Islands!" he shouted.

Agnes sighed and muttered, "Well, shit." But aside from

the rather ominous name, I had no idea why this was such bad news.

"And how many guards does he have?" Ma'at pressed.

Anhur shook his head and through gritted teeth answered, "I don't know."

Ma'at finally released his arm and stood by her father again. "I should take him with me. He's guilty of unspeakable crimes, and Anubis should hand out his punishment accordingly."

"Agreed," Ra said. "And as for the others who surrendered—"

But whatever fate Ra had intended for Anhur's conspirators remained known only to him. Although I still kept the sword pressed to the back of his skull, Anhur swiftly dropped to one knee, pulled a dagger from his boot, raised his arm, and plunged it into his father's chest. Ra's eyes widened and his mouth fell open as his hands touched the hilt of the dagger protruding from his body. I thought I heard Ma'at screaming for her father, and she most likely was as she clutched frantically at his body, trying desperately to keep him upright as if he could only stay on his feet, he could survive.

But Ra didn't stay on his feet.

He slumped forward, and Ma'at gently lowered him to the ground, her anger and pain so intense, her skin had taken on that crimson glow her brother had experienced earlier, only I doubted she was in physical pain.

But this kind of pain was far, far worse.

I knew because I'd experienced it before.

I don't remember killing Anhur. I only learned of it later, when Keira told me everything that happened after Ra's murder by his son. We'd been right that Anhur's death would lift the curse on Houston, but I have no memory of that either. The only thing I remembered was staring at Ra's body, feeling overwhelmingly guilty that I'd allowed Anhur to live long enough to kill a god I'd reluctantly come to consider a friend, and feeling guilty that I'd ever disliked him just because I felt threatened by him, even though Keira had never shown any romantic interest in him.

And Ra's death, this powerful sun god, one of the most important gods in his pantheon if not the entire world of the ancient gods, was dead.

If gods like him could be killed so easily, what chance did the rest of us have? What chance did my friends, my great-uncle, my Valkyrie, have in surviving a conflict with a god who was convincing mortals to surrender their souls to him?

And it might have only been my grief, my shock, my imagination, but I thought Havard whispered, *"None, Gavyn. We may have already lost this world."*

CHAPTER ELEVEN

Reykjavik, Iceland hadn't changed at all since my training days. Granted, it had only been a couple of months, but still. I was pretty sure we even had the exact same hotel rooms. Our team had thinned considerably, though, and being back in the place where my hero's journey had begun served as a painful reminder that we'd lost Tyr, that Thor was still in the hospital, and that Freyja had lied to us all from the beginning. But really, *all* of the gods had been lying to me the whole time. They'd known Havard's far more powerful genes could subsume my personality forever, and no one had been willing to tell me the truth. If I *had* known, would I even still be here?

Agnes had just broken the news about Ra's death to Joachim, Frey, Ull, Cadros, and Nuada, and the hero and gods looked defeated already. We hadn't even told them yet about Ninurta and the human sacrifices, *or* that he'd wisely chosen to hide on an island that was almost impossible to get to.

"Anubis took Ra's body home," Agnes said. "I don't think he'll be returning. Ra's loss is devastating to the Egyptians."

Frey nodded and sighed then rubbed his eyes with the

heels of his hands. He looked exhausted, like he'd been the one who'd recently survived nine circles of Hell. "Inti and Mama Pacha have gone home as well," he said. "Peru is safe now, and after the curses placed on Baton Rouge and Houston, most gods have decided to stay out of this war. We're up against powers unmatched by almost every pantheon in the world."

"It gets better," I said. "Apparently, Ninurta is on some gods-forsaken island where all these dumbasses are sacrificing themselves to make him more powerful." And my sluggish brain *finally* realized, "Hey, if it's so difficult to get there, where are all these sacrificial dumbasses coming from?"

"They probably all traveled with him initially," Keira guessed.

"We need to confront him as soon as possible then," Nuada decided. "Once news reaches him that Anhur is dead, he'll likely move elsewhere, and we may never be able to find him."

"And waiting until he attacks *us* would be a huge mistake considering how powerful he could become," Ull added.

Frey glanced at me and sighed again. "I *really* wish you'd been able to find your sword. I'm not sure we can defeat him and Inanna without it."

"Hey," Agnes protested. "Speak for yourself. We Tuatha Dé don't need magical weapons to defeat our enemies."

Yngvarr blinked at her before asking, "*How* has your ego not gotten you killed yet?"

I pointed at my great-uncle and agreed. "What he said."

So Agnes squinted at me and snapped, "How has your stupidity not gotten *you* killed yet?"

"Another excellent question," I agreed again.

Havard had been silently moping—or grieving, I wasn't really sure—but he finally chimed in to remind me I had more important things to do than sit around a hotel room harassing my friends. "*You should go to Syracuse, Gavyn. This is the beginning of the end.*"

"God, you're like the Riddler," I mumbled aloud.

"*I thought my instructions were pretty clear, actually.*"

I grunted at him but announced, "Apparently, I have to go to New York, because it's not like I *just* flew to Iceland and want to sleep off this jet lag or anything."

"What's in New York?" Frey asked.

I shrugged instead of telling him about my grandparents, because I already knew they didn't have my sword, so why the hell *was* Havard sending me there? And go figure—he apparently forgot how to speak again since I didn't get an answer.

"I'll go with you," Keira announced.

Frey immediately objected, not understanding why she'd want to go either, and he insisted they needed everyone together to prepare for Ninurta's final attack. But how could I tell her she *shouldn't* go to New York to see the man she'd raised as her son, even if she couldn't remember him?

"Look," I said, "we all know I shouldn't be trusted to go alone. Keira and I will run this errand for the pain in the ass god who's taken up residence in my brain—"

"*I haven't taken up residence in your brain,*" the pain in the ass god interrupted. "*I'm just a part of you.*" And for good measure, he threw in, "*Dumbass.*"

"And we'll be back in a few days," I finished, deciding to tell everyone now that the pain in the ass god who'd taken up residence in my brain was objecting to his residency just to annoy the hell out of him. I mean, he'd been annoying the hell out of me for months, so it only seemed fair.

"*That didn't even make sense,*" Havard pouted.

"*Yeah, well, they're used to me not making sense.*"

"Do you want me to go with you, too?" Yngvarr asked.

I understood his curiosity, this desire to reunite with family even though he wouldn't remember them, but those reunions would have to wait. "This needs to be as quick a trip as possible," I answered.

Agnes offered him a sympathetic smile and coyly suggested she'd help him pass the time, so I made an exaggerated retching sound and grabbed my duffel bag off the floor. I hadn't even *unpacked*. And if there's any doubt still that Havard could be such a dick, *that* moment should have cleared it up since he could've told me to go to New York *instead* of Iceland.

Not surprisingly, Havard didn't have anything to say about his late instructions.

On the flight back to the States, Keira kept a small notebook in her lap where she wrote tirelessly for almost an hour. I'd almost fallen asleep when she nudged me gently with her elbow and asked, "What does your grandfather like to do? Is he retired? From what?"

I opened a groggy eye but it didn't want to stay open. "Retired last year. Mostly, anyway. He was a history professor at Syracuse University. He still does some guest lecturing."

"A professor," Keira whispered.

Until I said it aloud, I hadn't even realized my grandfather had likely pursued his career in history because he'd *lived* through so much of it.

"And Clara?" Keira asked.

I sighed and gave up on trying to sleep. "She did something with old documents... like an archivist or something. What's with all the questions?"

Keira kept her attention on her notebook, and I stole a quick glance at what she'd scribbled on the page. Unfortunately, whatever she'd written wasn't in English and Havard, the bastard, refused to translate for me. "He'll remember me, Gavyn. Freyja's curse obviously didn't affect them since they had to teach your mother about your destiny, but he'll be a stranger to me. I won't know my own son."

I squirmed a bit because if he'd been her biological son, we would have a disgustingly Shakespearean relationship. "When I first met Yngvarr, I just kinda *knew* we had some special connection. Maybe it was just Havard reacting to his brother and that I'd been dreaming about this god I'd never even met, but I think it was more than that. I think no god, not Freyja nor Odin nor any of them, can really erase the ties we have to each other."

Keira smiled at her notebook and said, "Like Yngvarr and Agnes."

"Don't go there," I warned her. "I doubt I can make it to the bathroom in time to throw up."

She snorted and actually dug the barf bag out of the seat pocket in front of her.

"Smartass," I mumbled, but I took the bag from her anyway then added, "You know, if she and Yngvarr got married, she'd be like... my great-aunt. I'd have a *witch* for an aunt. And then their half-witch kids would be my cousins. Oh God, I hope Valhalla has Xanax."

"I don't think spirits have problems with anxiety," she said. "But if I'm wrong, I'll do my best to smuggle it in for you."

I laughed and closed my eyes again, foolishly thinking our conversation was over and I might actually get a chance to sleep for a while. As usual, I was wrong.

"Perhaps it won't matter though," she said quietly. "Even if we somehow defeat Ninurta and Inanna, Odin wants you dead and he wants the Sword of Asgard back in his possession. And he'll kill us all. I have no idea what will happen to you if you're not welcomed into Valhalla, or me if—"

I put my hand over hers and tried to lie, to promise I would protect her and I could win, not only against the Sumerians but *all* of the traitors in Asgard, but I couldn't lie to her. Not like this. So we sat in silence, holding onto each other's hands as a simple gesture of comfort, and somewhere over the Atlantic, we both fell asleep.

I awoke when the captain announced we'd be descending soon and the fasten seatbelts lights came back on. Now that we were over my home country, Keira looked nervous and her fingers actually trembled as they buckled her belt over her lap. Honestly, I was a bit nervous about confronting my grandparents, too. I mean, what if I showed up at their door and they treated me like I'd lost my freaking mind? What if they insisted everything I *thought* Havard had told me lately was a complete fabrication, and ultimately, they only confirmed what part of me had suspected all along? I really *was* going crazy and none of this, not even Keira and Yngvarr and Agnes or any of the extraordinary adventures I'd been on the past few months, were real.

"This was a bad idea," I muttered.

Keira glanced at me and arched an eyebrow. "Didn't Havard suggest we come here?"

I nodded and said, "It's just weird. These are my *grandparents*, people I've known and loved my whole life. And I'm about to confront them over having secret identities like they're superheroes or something."

"Or super-villains," Keira pointed out helpfully.

So, naturally, I agreed and said that *did* seem more likely. After all, I was descended from them.

We rented a car at the airport, and although Keira didn't mention Áki and our impending confrontation again, she was clearly nervous about it. We assumed, of course, he'd remember her and whatever vision of a five-year-old boy she'd created based on the stories I'd told her would be crushed by the reality that Paul was now a seventy-eight-year-old man.

I hadn't called ahead because I didn't want to risk tipping off any of our enemies that we were about to visit my grandparents, whom, as far as anyone else knew, were just a couple of harmless old people, so I was both relieved and anxious to see the lights on inside their house. As I pulled into the driveway, I took a deep breath and asked, "Are you ready?"

"I don't know him," she answered. "I have no memories of him at all. What if that hurts him? What if he thinks my love for him should have been stronger than Freyja's spell?"

"Then I'll know where I got my ability to be such an asshole," I said.

Keira snickered and opened her car door, her resolve far greater than mine, and we approached their front door as carefully as we'd approached each new circle of Hell. But unlike Houston, we didn't have to step through some magical gate or demarcation for the gatekeepers to come to us. Their front door opened before I could knock, and there stood Paul and Clara, the man and woman who'd pretended to be normal humans for at least twenty-seven years but probably far longer considering how much they'd aged. Living in Asgard would have preserved their youth. And neither looked overly surprised to see me.

"Gavyn," Paul said. "You've been on the news a lot lately."

I crossed my arms, suddenly angry that they'd *both* known this day would come and they'd kept me in the dark. Surely, at some point after my mom died, they could've told me the truth, prepared me or at least given me a heads up that I'd eventually be responsible for saving the world from a handful of the dickiest gods ever.

And if they *had* told me, it's not like I would have had them committed for senility or anything. At least, I *probably* wouldn't have.

My grandfather cast only the briefest glance in Keira's direction, but his expression remained unreadable. And it was only when I witnessed this briefest exchange between adopted mother and son that I realized Havard was seeing *his* daughter for the first time in a very long time.

I expected more emotion from him... surprise, excitement, nervousness, regret. *Something* to indicate any kind of intense emotional reaction to seeing his child in the twilight of her life. But when Havard remained as silently hidden as usual, when no new thoughts or feelings emerged that weren't mine, I *finally* understood another truth I'd been desperately trying to avoid since that first dream in Iceland about a young god who rode up to a small farmhouse and took the farmer's daughter as payment for a crime the family hadn't committed.

Havard hadn't suddenly appeared then, at this stage in my life where I had to become some hero I'd never wanted to be. He hadn't been activated within my DNA thanks to a supernatural crisis or any of the bullshit stories the gods had wanted me to believe, those gods who'd known this truth all along but had lied to me, who'd pretended to be in the dark about the rarity of such a deep connection between ancestor and descendant.

What they'd known all along, what I'd refused to acknowledge, was that Havard had *always* been a part of me.

Clara seemed to sense somehow that I'd just figured this all out, and she reached for me, but I wasn't ready to forgive her. Had she always known her father was in me, that he was sort of alive as long as I was? Had she spent the past twenty-seven years looking for signs of him instead of really seeing *me*?

"This was a bad idea," I muttered, backing away from the open door, but my freakishly strong Valkyrie grabbed my arm and refused to let me return to our rental car.

"They may be able to help us," Keira said softly, trying to comfort me, but I didn't want to be comforted. I wanted the one thing I couldn't have—my old life back. The life I'd always thought I'd had anyway.

But Keira pushed me back toward my grandparents, and Clara—or perhaps it was time to start thinking of her as

Astrid—grabbed my other arm and my seemingly feeble old grandma showed me just how much she'd been hiding from me, because that old woman was insanely strong, too.

I was half-pushed, half-pulled inside the house by, once again, an old lady and a young hot one.

I'd come full circle and, yeah, I was totally emasculated once again, especially since *this* old lady was my *grandmother*.

Paul locked the door behind us and tried to get my attention. "Gavyn," he said, "I know you feel betrayed, but—"

I turned on him and snapped, "You don't know *shit* about how I feel, *Áki*."

His eyes flickered to Keira again, and he swallowed but kept trying to reach for me. "If we'd told you, if your mom—" His words stuck in his throat, my first painful reminder that they'd lost their daughter, this beautiful, intelligent, vivacious woman. And all of my anger was temporarily replaced with this shared loss and unwavering sense of grief we'd always live with.

Paul cleared his throat and said, "Your mother insisted we wait for you to come to us. She said Arnbjorg wanted it that way because it would be safer for all of us. If Odin discovered we were the lost family of the rightful heir to Asgard's throne, we would have all been murdered. And I did make a promise to Havard long ago—"

"I know," I interrupted. "Any chance Mom ever told you how to get Havard to go radio-silent again?"

Clara arched an eyebrow at me and asked, "Do you really want him to right now?"

So I shrugged and replied, "He's kind of annoying."

She laughed and shrugged back, and for the first time since arriving, I felt Havard's presence as he reacted to his daughter's amusement. "*Tell her*," he begged, "*I still love her laugh*."

I grunted at him but relayed his message anyway. "You

know," I added, "in Havard's memories, it seemed like Mom was your first-born, but she was an only child... right?"

Clara and Paul glanced at each other, and I immediately knew I was about to discover a much deeper nest of lies that had formed the stories of my life.

"By the time we had to leave Asgard, all of our children were grown. We agreed it would be safer for our two younger sons to take different names and pretend they weren't related. You know them as your mom's old friends from grade school."

"Oh my God," I groaned. "Dave and Zack are my *uncles?*"

My grandma actually looked a little offended that I seemed insulted by my relation to her sons, and Havard cautioned me—a little too cheerily—to be careful since she'd inherited the family temper.

"*You* be careful," I mumbled back at him, but Paul and Clara weren't used to me talking aloud to a voice in my head like Keira and my godly friends were, so they both asked me if I needed to lie down for a while. And my grandma even felt my forehead like she was checking for a fever as a possible cause of my delirium.

Apparently, she'd inherited the smartass gene as well.

I stepped back and narrowed my eyes at her and, for good measure, at my grandfather. "What about Dad? How much did he know? Has no one in my life been honest with me?"

Paul shook his head and assured me, "He never knew any of this. He really did meet your mother in college, and even if she'd wanted to tell him the truth, how could she without him thinking he'd fallen in love with a crazy person?"

I slowly exhaled, relieved that I hadn't been alone in my ignorance but also relieved that my dad, at least, had never been part of this fabricated life.

"And Mom," I said, my voice sounding so small, like a twelve-year-old boy's. "Was she...?" What was I trying to ask?

What did I really want to know about the woman I'd loved so much, the woman for whom I still mourned, the woman who'd taught me what *real* strength and courage were? In the end, the only question that came out was, "You all changed your names. Did she?"

Clara blinked back tears and lowered her eyes but nodded. "Yes," she whispered. "We'd named her Hjordis."

My mouth fell open to ask them what the hell they'd been thinking, but Havard answered before I had the chance. *"It means sword goddess,"* he explained. *"They knew her fate as the mother of the man who would inherit my sword."*

Hjordis. My mother's name had been Hjordis.

I didn't care how fitting the name had been; she'd been given a raw deal in the naming department, and the one good thing to come from their exile was that she no longer had to go by *Hjordis*.

"I'm sure Gavyn has a million questions," Keira interjected, "but we really need any information you can give us as to where his sword may be hidden."

Paul looked at her again, and I finally saw how much he'd missed her, how desperately he wanted to hug her, to remind her how grateful he was for being saved all those centuries ago, for being loved as her son. "Gunnr," he said, so of course I had to correct him.

"It's Keira now."

"*He* can call me Gunnr," she said, correcting *me*.

Quite naturally, I crossed my arms again and pouted.

And, just as naturally, Havard thought that was hilarious.

"Unfortunately, we don't know exactly where it is," he replied, flashing me a mischievous grin as he emphasized, "*Gunnr*. But it wouldn't be with anyone related to Havard. Yngvarr, their sisters, even Finn. Odin would've suspected them all and already searched their palaces."

"Wouldn't Havard know?" Clara asked me.

"If he does, he's being a total dick about it, which actually wouldn't surprise me."

"*I sort of know. And I already told you that,*" he reminded me.

I threw my hands up and exclaimed, "You only said it was in Asgard!"

"That must get really annoying," Paul said to Keira. Not *me*, the one with the dead god in his head who wouldn't shut up, but Keira.

"*Gavyn, I've been with you since your birth. I suspect certain things because Arnbjorg has told me—*"

"Whoa," I interrupted. "*You can communicate with your dead wife even though you're hanging out in* me? *And does that mean Arnbjorg was hanging out in my mom? Wait, that sounds like a really bad porno. Let me try again.*"

Havard sighed irritably and didn't give me the chance to rephrase my questions. "*No, Arnbjorg couldn't be partially reincarnated in your mother, because she was born long before we died* and *she's fully human. But that's why we don't actually know for sure if we're right about where we* think *the sword is. And life after death is complicated, Gavyn. I can be a part of you, and I can be elsewhere, too. What kind of afterlife would it be for me if I were permanently separated from Arnbjorg? What kind of afterlife would it be for you if you never saw Keira again?*"

"It would be Hell," I immediately answered. "*And not Odin's recreation of Dante's Hell but actual Hell... if an actual Hell exists. But even if it doesn't, that would be it.*"

"*Exactly. Now would you just ask your grandparents if there's anyone in Asgard your mother trusted wholeheartedly that she's* not *related to?*"

I wanted to fixate some more on my mom and my great-grandparents and where they were, but I obeyed because, honestly, the conversation was also kinda freaking me out. "What about friends?" I asked. "Did mom have any friends in Asgard that she would have trusted with something like this?"

Paul and Clara's eyes lit up and my grandma said, "Yes, her childhood best friend. Freyja's daughter, Tova."

"You have *got* to be kidding me," I complained.

"You can say that again," Keira agreed.

"Freyja *saved* us with that curse and even helped us pass for a normal human family by aging Astrid and me twenty years so we'd *look* old enough to have college-aged kids," Paul said, thinking Keira was only reacting to her old animosity with the war goddess rather than the much newer one. And since I didn't want her to tell my grandparents all about my colossally stupid mistake, I hurriedly asked, "But Odin would've known about Tova and... *Hjordis*. He would have suspected she might know something about the sword, too, right?"

"Odin knew about Hjordis but nothing about her life," Clara answered. "He wasn't in Asgard the entire time, not until the day we were forced to leave. And once Freyja's curse took effect, no one remembered your mother so how could Odin have discovered their friendship?"

"But if no one remembered Mom, why would Tova have agreed to help her?" I asked.

"Ask Freyja," she said. "I suspect she intervened somehow if Havard is so convinced Tova can help you."

"All right," I sighed, then to Keira said, "I guess we should go to Asgard and find out if Mom ever gave Tova anything to hide."

Keira offered me a weak smile then lowered her eyes as she said, "Paul, I..." But she faltered and shook her head, unsure how to tell an old man goodbye, especially one who shouldn't have grown so old and one whom she *should* remember as the boy she'd raised.

"Gunnr," he said. "For whatever it's worth now, you were the best mother I could've hoped for. And if anyone is going to be by our grandson's side in these battles, I'm glad it's you."

Keira smiled at some invisible spot on the carpet and grabbed my hand.

"Goodbye, Áki," she whispered then my grandparents' living room disappeared as we crossed the veil into Asgard in our last, desperate attempt to find the Sword of Secrets and Light and Prophecy, the Sword of Asgard that would allow me to defeat Ninurta and save the world.

CHAPTER TWELVE

"Freyja's daughter," Keira muttered as we stood in front of Freyja's palace. We figured we might as well enlist the goddess's help again in case her daughter was uncooperative. Plus, we had no idea what would happen if I *did* get my hands on the sword. Would Odin immediately know? Would he storm into Asgard or follow me on Earth to kill me before I even had the chance to confront Ninurta?

Since Keira was awfully busy glaring at Freyja's door, which was obviously a remarkably good use of our time, I knocked and hastily prepared a supplicatory request for her assistance. And, yeah, "supplicatory" was totally Havard's word, not mine.

But when Freyja opened the door and ushered us inside, it quickly became clear I wouldn't have to beg for her help after all.

"What's wrong?" she asked. "Is Frey all right?"

"For now," I assured her. "But considering Ninurta is empowering himself with human sacrifices, we may *all* be screwed." I filled her in on everything we'd recently learned—

from Anhur *and* my grandparents—as well as Ra's death. And by the way her face fell when I mentioned Ra's murder, I deduced *he* was one of her past lovers as well, so I quickly changed the subject, both for her benefit *and* mine.

"Tova... do you think my mom might have asked her to hide the sword?"

Freyja lifted a shoulder and said, "It's definitely possible. They'd been inseparable since toddlerhood. When your mom —" Freyja sighed and touched my arm, which made Keira tense up, but I didn't pull away from the war goddess. The twelve-year-old boy in me who still cried for his mother every single day wanted to know each memory, each experience, each cherished thought of the most extraordinary woman who'd ever lived. "Tova never stopped mourning," Freyja finished. "Friends like that... they can't ever be replaced."

"So Tova still remembers her?" Keira asked, somehow managing to look both pissed off that Freyja's hand was still on my arm and genuinely curious about Freyja's explanations.

"She remembers Hjordis, but nothing about Havard and Arnbjorg. How could I have taken my daughter's best friend from her?"

"If she has my sword, will Odin know somehow it's in my hands? Will he come after me?" I asked.

"He'll know," Freyja confirmed. "But I may be able to buy you some time. I can put a cloaking spell on you and everyone you're fighting with so he won't be able to find you. I'm afraid he'll eventually figure out how to work around it, but it may give you enough time to reach Ninurta and Inanna."

"Don't guess you have a teleportation spell," I said. "Because reaching him may be a bigger challenge than killing him."

Keira stood up straighter and exclaimed, "I think I know

how we can get there. Are you still completely opposed to riding a winged horse?"

I blinked at her and when that didn't elicit a different response I tried squinting. When she *still* just stared back at me like I was deep in my role as village idiot, I snapped, "We need serious suggestions here. Like stealing a helicopter."

Keira folded her arms over her chest and snapped back, "*That's* a serious suggestion? Can you even *fly* a helicopter?"

"No, but I can't fly Pegasus either."

She waved me off and said, "He's not Pegasus. For God's sake, Gavyn, we'd never fly a *Greek* horse."

"*That's* what you took away from my complaint? That this whole resistance to flying a winged horse has anything to do with its heritage?"

"Just hold onto the reins," she insisted. "He won't let you fall. And it's not like we have any other options, so stop whining."

And since she'd only told me to stop whining and had said nothing about pouting, I crossed my arms, too, and pouted instead.

"What about your new friends in the FBI or CIA or whatever agency Frey was working with?" Freyja asked. "Why don't you just call them? Surely, they have quite a few helicopters at their disposal."

"We can't risk their lives like that," Keira argued. "No mortal would get off that island alive. As it is, we're only going with a couple of demigods, the ones who've demonstrated they can handle a battle of this magnitude. The rest will stay with Agnes's sisters in case there are any more diversions."

"Sounds like we're taking the winged horses then," Freyja said to me, and she even shrugged like it was no big deal to ride a huge mammal that shouldn't be flying.

"Besides," Keira added in one of her extremely rare

moments of solidarity with her arch-rival, "they'd hear the helicopters approaching. They won't hear our horses."

"A Pegasi sneak attack sounds like a *brilliant* idea," I teased, and both Havard and Keira told me Pegasi wasn't a word and yeah, it *was* a brilliant idea. But Havard also added, *"So stop whining and man up. Even my kids didn't complain this much when they were actually kids."*

"*You* man up," I mumbled aloud. Honestly, I didn't even know what that was supposed to mean.

"So," Freyja said slowly, "can I cast the spell and take you to Tova's now?"

"Please," Keira begged. "The faster, the better, because I'm afraid if I ask him what 'manning up' means, I'll have to kick his ass."

And even though I was still pouting, I just had to retort, "The faster the better? That's the first time I've ever heard that."

Keira blinked at me then turned back to Freyja. "Like I said: the faster the better."

Freyja nodded like they were suddenly good friends in some anti-Gavyn secret sorority and said, "Have the Valkyries ready in case Tova has the sword. If Gavyn gets his hands on it, you'll want to leave as soon as possible."

"I'll meet you at Tova's then," Keira replied. "And we'll have an entire army of Valkyries ready to go."

"Wait," I exclaimed, and she turned around like I was actually going to say something important, but that was on her. She should've known better by now. "Pretty sure Havard was referring to my age, not my gender, considering all of the most badass warriors we know are women."

"You stopped me for that?" she sighed.

I shrugged and pointed out, "Didn't want you to kick my ass or think I didn't have all the respect in the world for you."

Keira actually smiled at me and promised she'd join us

soon, but miraculously, I'd managed to unpiss her off about the whole "manning up" thing, so I followed Freyja out of her palace feeling a bit victorious and more than a little *manly*.

But Tova apparently lived close by so when I realized just how little time I'd have to ask Freyja about my mother, I dropped my whole puffed out chest thing and scrambled to come up with the questions I most wanted answered.

And I came up with, "So you knew my mom?"

I thought I heard Havard sigh and mumble, "*Dumbass*."

By the way Freyja looked at me, she completely agreed with my great-grandfather. "Obviously. And she was... luminous, Gavyn."

"Yes," I agreed. "She was." I glanced toward Valhalla where I'd soon be taking up my permanent residence and lifted my chin in its direction. "Once I end up there, will you come tell me stories about her?"

Freyja offered me a strained smile and nodded. "Of course." But her smile turned sly and she added, "If Keira will let me."

I snickered then thought about it and also agreed, "Right. If she lets you." But the more I thought about it, the more I had to know if Freyja had known all along Keira and I were destined to fall in love and if she'd seduced me anyway. Sure, it was my own damn fault for giving in, and she clearly had a long, contentious history with my Valkyrie, but had she not cared at all about how it would affect *me*? "Freyja," I said, slowing down just enough to buy myself enough time to find out the truth once and for all. "When you... when *we*..." I sighed and just dove in. "Did you always know Keira and I were meant to be together?"

Freyja kept her focus on her daughter's palace, and I thought she was going to avoid my question altogether, but if there was one thing I could say about this complicated goddess, it was that she owned up to her actions—good *and* bad. "Yes," she responded.

"But you came into my room anyway, knowing how much friction it would cause Keira and me."

"Yes," she responded again.

I exhaled angrily and demanded, "Why?"

She looked me over quickly then lifted a shoulder. "Because you remind me so much of Havard. Not the way you act, but you look so much like him. For a brief moment, I was able to pretend like I was with him."

"That is the most messed up thing I've ever heard," I snapped. "You used me to live out some fantasy with my dead great-grandfather?"

"Gavyn," she sighed, "you could have said no. You could have thrown me out of your room, but you didn't. You can either let this go or spend the rest of eternity resenting me for loving the one god I could never have. Either way, it only really affects you, so I'd advise you to choose wisely."

We'd reached Tova's palace, and while Freyja was right, I decided to hang onto my anger just a little bit longer, even if I had to hide it since I *did* need her help. But from what I remembered about that night, I'd seemed under a spell, like I had little agency and *had* to accept. Whether it was the enchanted ring, which I still didn't want, or a spell of her own, I hadn't *felt* in control. Or maybe that was just a lie I kept telling myself thanks to this guilt that I'd almost ruined the chance to be with the one woman I'd never be able to get over if I'd lost her.

And it's not like Freyja gave me the chance to stand around pondering my past mistakes. She knocked on Tova's door, and a goddess who looked remarkably like Freyja answered and invited us inside. Although Tova's palace was smaller than her mother's, it was decorated in the same lavish style with the same obsessive collection of opulence and grandeur. And she also had her mother's seductive smile that made me wish Keira would hurry the hell up. I mean, I was her best friend's son. Shouldn't that have made me off-limits?

"Gavyn," Tova purred. "You're even more handsome than I've heard."

I stammered a bit and tried praying to any god who would listen that Keira would get her ass over here *now*. And at least one god *was* listening and thought it was a good time to remind me that if I weren't such a dumbass, I wouldn't have to feel so awkward around Freyja or her daughter.

I told that god to shut up but doubted he would ever listen.

But another god—one who wasn't *nearly* as annoying as the dead guy living in my body—must have heard my prayer as well, because Keira appeared in the doorway behind me and announced, "The Valkyries are ready."

I gaped at her and asked, "*All* of them?"

Keira just smiled and shrugged at me like I shouldn't have been surprised that every single one of Odin's slaves, who also happened to be his *daughters*, was ready and eager to rebel against their father even without their memories of his attack on Asgard and betrayal of everyone he was supposed to lead.

"So," Freyja said to her daughter, "we're hoping you can lead us to an extremely important package Hjordis might have left in your care for her son."

Tova glanced at me again and flashed another smile in my direction that was still far too suggestive for my comfort. But she waved us on and whispered, "This way," as if the walls themselves had ears. Hell, this was Asgard—maybe they did.

We followed her to an impressive library, the kind I'd expect to see in movies with aristocrats who lived in castles, but a huge part of me just couldn't get excited about whatever Tova had hidden for me. I mean, after everything I'd been through, it *couldn't* be this easy. There was no way I could just walk into someone's library and find the Sword of Asgard.

Which reminded me...

"Keira, the sword we found in Odin's palace belonged to my grandparents. Havard gave it to Arnbjorg, and I'm almost positive they gave it to Astrid and Áki when they married. How do you think Odin got that sword?"

Keira shook her head. "No idea. They're still alive, so we know he didn't kill them for it."

"I know," Freyja said. "When they left Asgard, they left everything behind that could identify them on Earth as Astrid and Áki. I was the one who advised them to. When they vanished, Odin ransacked their palace then had it razed to the ground, but by that time, no one could remember them and had no idea they were destroying a home a family had so recently occupied."

Tova urged us to follow her, unconcerned about ancient history, but to me, none of this was history at all. It was my life, playing out in the present no matter when any one of these events took place. So we continued to follow her, but I whispered to Keira, "This probably isn't my sword. I wouldn't get your hopes up." By the way she gripped my elbow as we wove between enormous shelves filled with leather-bound books, I doubted she shared my reservations though.

Tova stopped in front of a full shelf and began to pull volume after volume off, laying them carefully on a nearby table. Her mother helped her, and soon, we were staring at an empty bookcase with a stone wall behind it. Tova motioned for me to join her and said, "Come help me, Gavyn. We need to move this bookcase out of the way."

Now, sure I was a demigod and everything, so I was stronger than a normal human, but the damn thing looked like it weighed a thousand pounds. But I thought, "Eh, what the hell... might as well throw my back out right before battling one of the douchiest gods in history."

Keira grabbed the same side and, together, we managed to push the ridiculously heavy bookcase away from the wall. Miraculously, we didn't even hurt ourselves, which I attributed to some Asgardian magic. But we were still staring at a solid stone wall, so I shot Tova my best, "You'd better have some *more* Asgardian magic to make a doorway appear somewhere," look, which was a really hard look to master, and I even put my hands on my hips to indicate my impatience.

Tova shot me her own look, which I translated as, "Be patient," with an added, "Dumbass," for emphasis, and ran her fingers along a perfectly ordinary stone, nearly identical to the others on the wall.

Her fingertips found the seam where it had been sealed in place, and she tugged gently on it while murmuring softly to herself. Havard grew excited, and his nervous energy became contagious. How could it not? He was a part of me.

Tova finished her incantation, and the stone slowly slid out of place, revealing a narrow, dark tunnel just large enough for hiding some kind of treasure, like an irreplaceable and invaluable sword. She reached inside and pulled a long, heavily wrapped bundle from its hiding place, laying it on the floor in front of me.

"This," Tova said, "is what your mother entrusted to me with specific instructions to tell no one about it and to only remove it when you came for it. For over fifteen years, I've had no idea what's inside and I've kept my promise to her."

I blinked at the bundle by my feet, but I didn't pick it up. I didn't unwrap it. It wasn't the possibility—or even the likelihood—that the Sword of Asgard had been hidden inside this package. I was frozen in place because my mother, the woman who had been more goddess than human, had brought this here. For me. I was paralyzed by the knowledge of how much *faith* she'd placed in me, her belief—her *certainty* —that I would one day change the world.

She'd known this all along, and she'd always tried to assure me that I *could*.

Keira put her hand in mine and reminded me I wasn't alone. And my mother's faith in me shouldn't be wasted now.

She knelt on the floor and I mimicked her, still feeling as if my body and my mind were disconnected, but I helped her remove what appeared to be one of our old tablecloths. When I found the saucer-sized purple stain from spilling my grape juice—give me a break, I'd only been seven—I knew. Not that this had been our tablecloth I thought she'd thrown out, but that this final gift from my mother was the sword she'd once been given by her grandfather so long ago, the Sword of Asgard with which I was destined to save the world, even at the expense of my own life.

And it was that moment I was truly, finally okay with dying, with sacrificing myself for the good of others. And if that made me a hero, I'd wear that title proudly.

Beneath my mother's tablecloth were layers of papers that been taped together, and as I pried one loose, Havard's excitement over seeing his sword again transformed into something wholly different. I couldn't quite place this emotion, or really, this bundle of emotions, which were as tightly woven together as the sword's casing had been.

I flipped the colorful page over and recognized it but couldn't place it at first. In my mind, my great-grandfather whispered, "*The book of our ancestors' stories that Arnbjorg once brought me and asked me to read to her. The day she asked me if I were in those legends. The day she told me she loved me.*"

"Oh," I breathed aloud. "Why would Mom have used these pages? Is it a clue? Is it supposed to mean something?"

Havard was quiet for so long, I thought the reminder of

this powerful love he'd shared with my great-grandmother had caused him to shut down, to wall himself away from me so I couldn't pry into his personal pain. But Keira, understanding there was a special significance to these beautifully illustrated pages, continued to remove them carefully and pile them neatly on the floor next to us.

"*I think,*" Havard finally said, "*she wanted you to know that we're all connected. Forever, regardless of time or worlds or even death. Our connections are permanent, a part of us, and they can never be broken.*"

I swallowed an aching burning in the back of my throat as Keira pulled the final pages away from the sword I'd seen so many times in my dreams and in my memories that I had every engraving, every rune and curve, etched into each cell of my body, just as it had been for my great-grandfather so long ago. And even though I didn't need his confirmation, I asked him anyway. "*Is it...?*"

"*Yes,*" he said, his voice quivering as he urged me to pick up my sword.

I smiled to myself and nodded to the familiar rune on the hilt. "*Your sword, Havard. I just need to borrow it.*"

"*Pick it up, Gavyn,*" he ordered again.

Everyone in the room had been staring at me, waiting for this moment, and so, for once in my life, I willingly complied with someone's order. As I reached for the Sword of Asgard, I heard Keira and Freyja inhale sharp breaths like they expected some explosive display of magic or for all any of us knew, maybe even an actual explosion.

My fingers brushed against the silver hilt and traced Havard's symbol before wrapping around the handle and lifting the sword from the floor.

And part of me—okay, all of me—was incredibly disappointed when nothing happened. I shot a strained smile in

Keira's direction and stood up, telling her, "Well, I guess we should—"

But I never got the chance to finish my extremely unheroic speech about how we should go get our asses kicked. Because the sword began to glow, not faintly like in my dream when it alerted Havard to nearby dangers, but a brilliant, blinding light that forced us to close our eyes until the room dimmed once more. Beside me, Keira gasped, "I remember."

I opened my eyes and arched an eyebrow at her. "You remember what?"

Her wide eyes met mine and she breathed, "Everything."

"Everything," I repeated.

The curse.

It had been broken when the Sword of Secrets was back in the hands of its rightful heir.

I loosened my grip on the hilt and stared at the sword, blinking once, twice. Maybe my retinas had been burned after all.

But Keira reached over and ran a fingertip along a rune that had never existed on this sword before. Havard's symbol was gone. And in its place was one I didn't recognize, and yet, I knew it.

The Sword of Asgard was mine.

Freyja's head snapped up like she'd heard something alarming, and she grabbed my arm, urging me to hurry. "You have to go now. All of Asgard remembers Havard and the war that almost destroyed us, which means those old rivalries will resurface. And those who supported Odin will come looking for you."

I had at *least* a million and one questions about their restored memories and this battle between Havard and Odin and who had allied with whom. I mean, if there were someone *I'd* been allying with, shouldn't I know he or she might stab me in the back now? But Freyja was already pushing me out the door, promising she'd be joining us soon to help us in the upcoming battle with Ninurta and Inanna because we'd need all the help we could get.

But even as Freyja pushed me back toward the front of Tova's palace, it seemed to be fading, replaced with violently crashing waves against a rocky beach. Ninurta and Inanna stood on a cliff top overlooking that beach while a young man, whose bare chest heaved in deep, nervous breaths, waited in front of them.

The blade of Ninurta's knife reflected the sunlight and I tried to squeeze my eyes shut again so I wouldn't witness this sacrifice. But the coast and this island and the gods who were about to murder a man simply to make themselves more powerful weren't really in front of me, so closing my eyes did nothing to stop the sacrifice from occurring. But the scene didn't end there. The Sword of Prophecy was showing me my future.

It was telling me two things: one, every god we'd fought before, even the Mesopotamian gods who'd first appeared with Ninurta and Inanna, had been nothing more than diversions. All this time, they'd kept us distracted while these two made themselves powerful enough to take over the world and to defeat whatever assemblage of heroes and gods we could throw together.

And it had worked. We'd followed the trails of destructions across continents, trying to save as many lives as possible while the real threats, the only ones that would matter in the end, had enacted the plan they'd had all along.

But more importantly, my sword was showing me that I shouldn't abandon all hope. Not yet. Because there *was* a path to victory, and as I'd been told all along, it would depend on me.

A bright light snapped me out of my vision. We'd stepped outside where every Valkyrie in Asgard—at least forty of them—waited atop their winged horses. Keira's sisters each had the same expression: they remembered everything now, too. And even though I didn't yet know what had happened during Asgard's civil war, I could tell their fight against Odin was no longer just about freedom.

It was about revenge.

CHAPTER THIRTEEN

All of the Valkyries' winged horses immediately crossed the veil just like we did, but since we returned to our starting point on Earth—a hotel in Reykjavik, Iceland—we had a bit of a space problem. And those winged horses didn't seem to like the narrow hallways of a cramped hotel. Keira held two reins, one for her horse and one for mine, but I was still in denial that I'd be *riding* a flying horse into battle. I mean, fighting devil dogs and gods who could transform into lions was one thing, but I had to draw a line *somewhere*, and I thought this was as good a place as any... mostly because I was a bit afraid of heights.

Okay, a lot afraid of heights, and more specifically, *falling* from those heights.

Not all of the horses could even fit in the hallway, so we assumed they'd crossed the veil and ended up outside, and as Keira handed the reins over to one of her sisters so we could share the news with our friends about the Sword of Asgard and her strategy to reach Ninurta and Inanna, I witnessed something that threatened to psychologically damage me for the rest of my short life. And my extremely long afterlife.

One of the doors was slightly ajar, and my first thought was that we were already too late even though we'd arrived only minutes after we found the sword. Heart racing, sweat beading along my forehead, praying my friends and especially my great-uncle were okay, I pushed the door open and charged in.

And that's when I saw it.

Agnes and Yngvarr groping and kissing each other and tugging at clothes like horny teenagers. "You have *got* to be kidding me!" I scolded.

Yngvarr stopped kissing her long enough to look in my direction, and he arched an eyebrow and gave me a mischievous grin. "*You* broke the curse. Not our fault we remember now that we've been madly in love for centuries."

"First of all, ew," I retorted. "Secondly, you're welcome. Thirdly, you suddenly remember your dead brother and sister-in-law, and *this* is how you react? And fourthly, get off her because I'm useless to this world if all I'm doing is retching or gouging out my eyes."

Agnes sat up and scolded me back. "You are *such* a baby."

So I nodded seriously, because there were some things that just demanded infantile behavior and this was definitely one of those things.

Yngvarr shrugged at me and answered, "You weren't here, so you missed the shock of suddenly having our memories restored because you were in Asgard. Believe me: we *all* felt it. And you should know better by now that of course I miss my brother and his wife, but I wasn't as taken aback by their murders as you might think. I knew about his prophecy, even if I refused to believe him for the longest time. And I suspect there are still a few things Havard hasn't told you."

I crossed my arms and scowled at him, but really, it was only because I couldn't scowl at Havard. "What is *that* supposed to mean?"

"He'll tell you when he's ready."

"I'm so sick of this family's cryptic bullshit," I complained.

Yngvarr just shrugged again and promised me he and Havard were just trying to help me the best way they knew how, but honestly, it just felt like some asshole was trying to drag out the suspense of our story, which was *such* a dick move.

Keira pulled me from their sex room to the adjoining one where the other gods were still discussing their restored memories, the truths they'd been forced to forget, and what would happen to Asgard in the end. Odin had already demonstrated he'd do anything to keep the throne, and the civil war Havard had largely averted by sacrificing himself could play out in all its destructive ferociousness now.

At the first lapse in conversation, Keira shared her plan to reach the Sumerians, but none of those traitorous bastards objected to riding flying horses, which meant persisting in *my* objection would be wasted effort. In fact, they all thought her plan was brilliant since Grande Terre was so difficult to reach by conventional modes of transportation.

Yngvarr slipped into the room and kept shooting me weird looks, so I returned them even though I had no idea why he was looking at me like that in the first place. But anytime I had the chance to look at someone like they were on the verge of becoming a sociopath, I was going to take it.

In the midst of their battle planning, Yngvarr blurted out, "I didn't get the chance to say this earlier. I'm sorry, Havard."

So, naturally, I squinted at him and said, "So *you* were the one who killed him."

Yngvarr sighed irritably and shook his head. "No, dumbass. *Firstly*, you were the one just giving me a hard time about not reacting more to remembering my brother, so this is *your* fault. And *secondly*, I'm sorry I couldn't save him. I'm sorry I wouldn't let him talk more about his prophecy in all those years leading up to his death. Maybe if I had, we could have come up with a different plan, one in which he didn't have to—"

And that annoyingly intrusive dead god who lived within me seized control of my body to stop his brother from wallowing in his guilt. "There was nothing you could have done, Yngvarr. It *had* to end this way. It wasn't the god who took my sword or even Odin but Fate, and she cannot be defeated. When she wills something, it must come to pass."

"*Dude!*" I protested. "*Knock it off and give me my body back!*" Then I thought about it and added, "*Okay, that sounded totally pervy.*"

I suspected Havard mumbled "*Dumbass*," but I was more than a little distracted by my attempts to force him back into his little corner.

"Havard," Agnes butted in. "Who *did* murder you? Do you know this god now?"

My head nodded and my first reaction was to chastise Havard once more, but I was terribly curious about his murderer as well, so I stopped fighting him and allowed him to tell his spellbound audience whatever he needed to.

"I know now because I recognized him when the Sumerians resurfaced," he said. "I suspect Ninurta sent a lackey to Asgard thirty-five years ago, because Zababa isn't important enough on his own for Odin to have struck any sort of deal with him."

"Zababa," Yngvarr repeated, and both Havard and I didn't like his tone, the darkness that fell over his face, his thoughts clearly turning to revenge.

"Now isn't the time to lose our focus, brother," Havard warned.

For a brief second, Yngvarr didn't seem to register that his brother was even talking to him, but he closed his eyes and took a deep breath, and Agnes put a hand on his shoulder, reminding him he still had something that made life worth living. When he opened his eyes, I recognized my great-uncle, and the anger that had almost taken over receded.

Joachim rose from his chair and pointed out an obvious question we'd all overlooked. "Odin has been at Thor's bedside as he recuperates. It should be simple enough to find out if he's returned to Asgard or is looking for Gavyn just by going to the hospital, right?"

"Okay," Agnes said slowly. "And if he *is* there, we'll be walking right into the lion's den."

"And if he's not?" Ull asked. "Does it matter now? We can't take on Ninurta and Odin at the same time. We need to concentrate on the Sumerians first since it is *this* world they're threatening. If we survive that encounter, we'll deal with Odin next."

Freyja finally arrived, and I did a double take as I noticed just how badass she looked. I'd never seen her without her multitudinous gold rings and bracelets and necklaces, but she'd traded in her ostentatious garments and accessories for dark, simpler clothes and a leather vest. Two swords were sheathed behind her back, making it somewhat easier to fly a winged horse, and a much smaller scabbard lay against her hip, the hilt of a bronze dagger protruding from its leather case.

I'd always had such a hard time imagining Freyja as a war goddess, this woman who coveted jewelry and beauty, but looking at her now, I was actually a bit intimidated by her. "My cloaking spell won't hold forever," she said. "If we're going to Grande Terre, we need to leave now."

Not surprisingly, her brother agreed with her, but I wasn't so sure. Joachim had a point—knowing where Odin was and trying to figure out just how much he knew could be advantageous for us, because if we showed up in Grande Terre and discovered he was there, too, we'd likely be slaughtered before any real fight could begin. Of course, my sword hadn't *shown* me Odin's presence, but prophecies *could* change as Tyr had so tragically taught me. And Havard also pointed out that sometimes, prophecies could be more figurative. Just because I'd seen Ninurta and Inanna on a cliff didn't mean I'd *literally* be fighting them on a cliff.

"How tired will your magic horses get if we fly them to Thor's hospital first?" I asked.

Keira blinked at me like I'd just asked the World's Dumbest Question, which was really saying something considering I was the World's Dumbest Man. "They can handle it," she finally answered. "But why would we risk going to the hospital first?"

"If Odin's still there, it may be the easiest place to defeat him," I argued.

"And if we don't get to Grande Terre before Ninurta sacrifices another dozen humans, we won't be able to defeat *him*," Freyja argued back.

Keira sighed and said, "I hate to say this, but Freyja's right. We've worked too hard and come too far to let Ninurta and Inanna slip away now."

"We've been playing their game the entire time," I said. "They've set the rules and we've been gullible enough to chase decoys all over the world. But I don't think this was ever really the Sumerians' game. I think it was Odin's. He struck a deal with them to kill Havard, and he's done it again to kill *me* so he can get his hands on this sword. Without it, no one will be able to take his throne from him."

"But Havard," Yngvarr stammered. "What could Odin have promised them in exchange for Havard's life?"

I shrugged and guessed, "Maybe the sword itself. That's why Inanna told me it was a Sumerian weapon. It was *supposed* to be after they killed Havard for Odin. And Zababa *did* take it after killing him. We only have it now because Agnes retrieved it from someone."

All eyes turned to Agnes so she shrugged as well and said, "I killed the god who had the sword. It wasn't Zababa, obviously, but whomever was carrying the sword was still in Asgard when I found him. And Yngvarr and I arrived shortly after Havard and Arnbjorg were killed, which means Zababa didn't enter your world alone. I think Odin brought in a number of Sumerian gods."

Freyja tapped her fingers against her thigh, her eyes narrowed in both hatred and concentration. "It would be possible for a god as powerful as Asalluhi to change the Sword of Asgard's magic, cast an entirely different enchantment on it to benefit them. Once the sword was out of Odin's way, he wouldn't have to fear losing his throne."

I still gripped the sword in my hand, and I loosened my fingers to study my symbol that had temporarily replaced Havard's. I was the rightful bearer of its power at the moment, but when I died, who would inherit this weapon? Who would displace the King of the Gods to become Asgard's new ruler?

Yngvarr, I thought. Who could possibly be a better god to lead the Norse than the brother of the slain king?

And despite feeling like I'd been thrust into a Shakespearean tragedy, I smiled at my sword, confident in Yngvarr's ability to rule fairly and justly, and relieved that he'd inherit Valhalla as well. If it were to become my permanent home, at least I'd be serving a god who deserved my loyalty.

"Why are you smiling?" Agnes asked. "Knock it off, you freak."

"*You* knock it off, you witch," I demanded back.

"*I'm* not smiling," she pointed out. "And even if I were, it wouldn't be at an inanimate object."

"Um," Nuada interjected. "Can we go to Grande Terre now? Have we officially put Odin on the backburner? Do we need to take a vote?"

"Only Gavyn and Joachim think it's a good idea to hunt down Odin first," Cadros replied. "And they're only demigods, so—"

"Dude," I interrupted, pointing my sword in his direction. "Finish that sentence, and you won't make it to Grande Terre."

Cadros lifted an eyebrow at me, but Keira saved him by insisting flying horses weren't exactly easy to hide and word would soon spread about the odd animals and their armed riders. And the last thing we needed was having to fight our way out of this hotel. Again.

And so, despite my best efforts to avoid it, I found myself atop a horse with long, feathered wings, which was more than a little awkward because I couldn't quite figure out where my legs were supposed to go and where my sword was supposed to sit and how the hell was this one-thousand-pound animal going to *fly* anyway?

Keira mounted her Norse Pegasus, shouting a command to take flight, and I may or may not have shrieked and grabbed onto my horse's neck with both arms as it obeyed. And if I *did,* I probably would've ridden that way for what felt like eight hundred years as we rose above the lowest clouds. The air definitely got thinner, which seemed *perfect* for a guy already on the verge of hyperventilating, and occasionally, I'd catch glimpses of the deep blue ocean beneath us. But mostly, I kept my eyes closed and my arms wrapped tightly around my horse's neck—assuming, of course, that's how I actually rode all the way to Grande Terre.

The Valkyries' horses were surprisingly fast, far faster than our jets, which also didn't help the aforementioned hyperventilating, and Joachim, who rode beside me, apparently thought he was Sigurd himself—the Germanic hero, not Havard's horse. I honestly expected him to lift his bow above his head and yell like a German Tecumseh leading his warriors into battle. He didn't, of course, but his enjoyment of our voyage across two oceans atop flying mammals that shouldn't have been flying and defied every law of physics known to man just made me feel like the baby Agnes so often accused me of being. But can you blame me? Not only was I on a flying horse, I was at an altitude and speed I shouldn't have been able to survive, and even though my brain kinda understood it was all part of Asgard's magic, the rest of me didn't care.

I have to admit, though, that the flying horses' navigation systems were top-notch, because with no spoken commands, they dipped below the clouds and an island appeared on the horizon. As we neared it, though, we began casting worried glances at each other. Something was different about Grande Terre than the pictures we'd seen online. Structures jutted from its landscape, yet this island was *supposed* to be mostly uninhabited.

It wasn't until we were basically on top of it that I recognized the labyrinthine pattern, the yellow mud-brick buildings punctuated with vivid blue mosaics.

Grande Terre had been transformed into Sumer III.

"How?" I asked, which was probably just a rhetorical "how" since I didn't actually expect anyone to have an answer.

But Agnes did. Her eyes turned to flames as bright as any star, and her nostrils flared as she glared at the new city below. "Neither Ninurta nor Inanna could have done this," she said. "And I doubt Odin was briefed on our experiences in

Sumer II in order to reconstruct the world that took Tyr's life."

The often creaky cogs in my brain began to turn as I caught onto what Agnes was suggesting. "Ninurta's parents," I guessed.

Agnes nodded. "Enki and Ninhursag betrayed us after all."

CHAPTER FOURTEEN

We landed outside the walls of Sumer III, but before Agnes could discuss *why* Ninurta's parents would have helped us to escape in the first place, I exclaimed, "There'd *better* not be any devil dogs in there."

She waved me off and said, "Of course there are."

I thought about it then decided, "Okay, you go in and kill all the mutant canines that are obsessed with me. I'll wait out here until you give me the go-ahead."

"Why help you escape Sumer II in the first place?" Keira asked, choosing to ignore me just like everyone else. "They had the chance to kill you all, yet they actually saved your lives. This *has* to be my father's spell."

But Agnes shook her head. "Asalluhi created the enchantments that tricked us all over Sumer II. And as a powerful god of magic, he was more of a liability to Ninurta than an asset. If their alliance broke down, Asalluhi could've challenged Ninurta's leadership. They *wanted* us to kill him. And we've suspected for a while now that they have some sort of deal with Odin, who's needed Gavyn to find the Sword of

Asgard. So letting us into Sumer II, killing Asalluhi, helping us escape... they engineered the whole thing."

"How do you know all this?" I asked her.

Agnes shrugged and answered, "Common sense."

I would have reminded her she was a *mean* witch if I hadn't agreed I often lacked that particular trait.

But Yngvarr snorted and added, "It's part of the powers of a war god to intuit certain things related to battle. I have the exact same suspicions as Agnes."

Cadros nodded, and okay, I'd actually forgotten he was a war god, too. I mean, it's Belatu-Cadros... can you blame me? Did you even remember he was *part* of this story?

"So Ninhursag has created a trap for us," I said. "I think this stupid sword is broken, because the prophecy it showed me didn't have a labyrinth filled with Hellhounds in it."

Before Havard could finish reminding me that prophecies could be tricky and weren't always meant to be taken at face-value, Keira shot me a sharp look and asked, "What prophecy? You never told me about any prophecy."

"I never had the chance," I protested. Truthfully, I *could* have found a few minutes to tell her about the vision I'd had in Tova's palace, but part of me worried that I could change the course of events by discussing it, by influencing her actions or anyone else's. So I'd kept it to myself, but standing in front of the wall of another Sumerian death-maze, I was no longer so sure that had been the right thing to do.

And now, we were basically in their world again, and I couldn't risk anyone overhearing the only strategy I had for defeating the god who'd declared war on my planet. "You've been saying all along you trust me to win this battle," I said. "So trust me."

Keira never even hesitated. "I trust you, Gavyn."

I turned back to the wall and took a deep breath. "I guess

we just need to figure out how to get inside now. Thor's not with us to break through this wall."

"He may not be *with* us even if he weren't in the hospital," Yngvarr said.

For some stupid reason—yeah, yeah, that stupid reason was my stupidity—I hadn't connected the dots. Thor was Odin's son: his loyal, faithful son. And he may have once fought against my family and contributed to my great-grandfather's murder. Yngvarr caught me staring at him and said, "When Odin returned to Asgard, Thor refused to fight against his father. But he refused to fight against us as well. He knew war would lead to Asgard's destruction, which is the only reason he didn't choose sides."

"If I get the chance to fight Odin," I said, "how many more friends will I lose? And if Odin *wins*, what will happen to me in Valhalla? Can he torture a spirit? Oh my God, I really am going to end up in Hell, aren't I?"

"That won't happen," Keira insisted. "We'll protect you."

All of the Valkyries nodded, but Odin was one of the most powerful gods in existence. How could they possibly protect me from *him*? I glanced at Freyja and flashed her a sheepish grin, asking, "Can I live in your Land of the Dead Heroes?"

"No," Keira answered for her.

I sighed and faced the wall again. That was one battle I'd always lose, so why fight it?

Heidi, one of the Valkyries whose real name I'd forgotten as soon as I'd heard it, approached the wall and tapped at the sturdy bricks. "They want us inside. The wall isn't to keep us *out* but to keep us *in*."

I groaned as I imagined being trapped inside Sumer III with the devil dogs all hissing my name, but this was it—this was what all my training and battling lesser gods and monsters had been building up to. This was my swan song, my Custer's Last Stand, my Waterloo... man, I needed better metaphors.

But all the Valkyries approached different segments of the wall, tapping the hilts of their swords against the bricks as if looking for a weakness, or for all I knew, maybe a doorbell. Behind us, the winged horses whinnied and stamped their feet as if reminding us we were *all* a bunch of dumbasses. Why didn't we just *fly* over the wall?

Agnes stroked her horse's neck and smiled at him but shook her head at me. "Can't fly over. We don't want to risk the slaughter of our only way off this island. And besides, I'm pretty sure they have some sort of barrier above their world."

I didn't see any barrier, only sky and a few light bluish gray clouds. But the war gods, including Havard, all had the same impression. Ninhursag had cast some sort of spell to prevent us from entering the city by any other route than the one *she* wanted us to use.

One of the Valkyries, one I recognized from that first meeting in a conference room in Reykjavik, Iceland, finally found the way into this new Sumer anyway. Her hilt knocked against a brick and a hollow echo greeted each strike. We instinctively held our weapons ready as she lowered her sword and pushed against the brick. Joachim stepped closer to me, an arrow nocked on his bow but his eyes fixed on the wall, and said, "I want to see my daughter again. Even if it's just one last time."

"You'll see her," I promised. "You'll watch her grow up and teach her how to be a total badass, and one day, she'll become the world's greatest archer with a dozen gold medals around her neck. And you'll be there to see it all."

Joachim's lips twitched into the faintest of smiles and he took a deep breath. "This is her world. I'd rather she lose me than her freedom."

The brick fell inside the wall and a faint blue light shimmered through the opening, spreading like a cancer as it reached its fingers across the pale yellow bricks until it had covered a section large enough for us all to walk through. We waited until the light dimmed, but we could see nothing inside Ninhursag's city but rocks and sand and grass as if it were just the island we'd expected to find.

But my Sword of Light reminded me that illusions were all around, and so were our enemies. The blade glowed, a brilliant yellow light, and I had the overwhelming feeling that I needed to lead us inside these walls. Keira and Joachim flanked me, and together, we led the way into Ninurta's final battle.

Much like the circles in Houston, stepping through Sumer III's walls revealed the world Ninhursag wanted us to see. One of the most surprising aspects of her city were the skyscrapers that appeared limitless in their height. Some formed narrow alleys, ensuring we'd have to walk in pairs to pass through them, while others allowed wider roads, most of which were paved with bright blue tiles. Those skyscrapers hadn't been visible from outside the walls, which seemed impossible. I doubted I'd ever get used to the way magic fooled our senses.

"So war gods," I said. "What is your supernatural intuition telling you now?"

Yngvarr didn't miss a beat. "It's telling me we're about to get our asses kicked."

I nodded in serious agreement and gestured toward the road closest to us. "This is like a yellow brick road scenario, isn't it?"

"Probably," Agnes said. "But after the tidal waves in Sumer II's narrow alleyway, I'll take my chances with the Wizard of Ur."

"Oz," I corrected.

"Ur," she corrected back. "It was a city in Sumer." She squinted at me then added, "Dumbass."

So, naturally, I waved her off and pretended like I'd known that all along even though I wasn't fooling anyone.

Keira stepped carefully onto the blue-tiled street, and I grabbed her arm, just in case the ground opened up and tried to swallow her or devil dogs materialized out of thin air. When nothing happened, I stepped onto the road beside her and our army of crusaders followed.

"Think we can call ourselves the Justice League?" I asked.

"No," Keira answered. "I think we'd get sued if we tried."

"How would they serve us?" I countered. "Most of us are going home to different worlds humans can't get to when this is all over. Or we'll be dead, and who's going to sue a dead guy?"

"It's still a no, Gavyn," Keira insisted.

"Okay," I said. "Crusaders of the Lost Sword?"

She nodded toward the sword in my hand and pointed out, "It's not lost anymore."

"Guess I missed the boat on that one."

"Besides," she added, "it's a bit derivative. Might also get us sued."

"Still willing to risk it," I said.

"Gavyn," Agnes sighed. "Please shut up."

She hadn't told Keira to shut up, just me. Granted, I'd started it, but still. "Fine," I said, "but don't think I won't come up with a name for our Band of Merry Men."

"First of all," Agnes snapped, "most of us aren't men. And secondly, stop stealing existing names."

"When we get stuck with a name like Warriors Against Flaming Zombie Monkeys, you've no one to blame but yourself," I claimed. But since she gave me a look that warned me she was three seconds away from turning *me* into a flaming zombie monkey, I shut up and kept walking toward the city's interior.

We hadn't gone far when I noticed the road wasn't a solid blue after all. Paler beige tiles had been mixed in among the bright blue, forming mosaics that wove between the impossibly tall skyscrapers.

Havard's voice screamed at me to stop, but just in case I was having a particularly village idiot-ish day, he seized control of my body and *forced* me to stand still. I held out my arms to block my allies as well, but I still had no idea what had alarmed my great-grandfather so much.

Of course, this was a world of magic and as I'd learned over and over recently, magic never kept us waiting long before trying to kill us.

The beige tiles flickered then rose from the road, immediately transforming again to reveal what had been in the mosaics all around us on the numerous roads between buildings.

"Lions," I breathed.

I vaguely remembered the mosaics from the Babylon we'd been transported to after the vampires attacked us in Baton Rouge and Thor had been so badly injured.

"Marduk," I hissed.

That bastard had betrayed us as well.

The lions roared at us as if hearing Marduk's name pissed them off, too, but Agnes was unconvinced. "Marduk may be more powerful than Ninurta. I'm not so sure they're working together, because Marduk would have the ability to overthrow Ninurta as soon as the world was in their control."

"They're half-brothers, though," I argued. "World domination is obviously a family business. His brother and parents are in this together, so why *not* Marduk?"

The last of the lions rose from the mosaics and with some silent, invisible signal, charged us. Ull's arrows released from his bow at dizzying speeds, with Joachim's following only a split second later.

The light from my sword reminded me I now had the gods' most powerful weapon in my hands, but I had no idea how to use it. But how hard could it be? Considering the arrows were only slowing down the spawn of the Nemean lion, the power of the sword *had* to save us... or we wouldn't survive Ninhursag's first assault.

I executed a rather impressive leap and slash maneuver at one of the lions, whose mane must've been made of steel, because my sword hit its neck hard enough to knock me on my ass yet didn't decapitate the bastard. In fact, it only pissed him off, and his alarmingly huge mouth loomed directly over my face.

I had no idea how she got to my side so quickly, but Keira was suddenly there, standing by the gargantuan lion that I swear was licking his lips—if lions *had* lips—in anticipation of devouring me. Keira held her sword in both hands and plunged it into the lion's back, yanking the blade back toward her. The lion turned its horrifying head to devour Keira, and I panicked. I didn't even notice my sword's light intensifying as I thrust it upward toward the lion's throat.

An explosive force burst from the blade, which just happened to be firmly entrenched in the lion's neck, and the supernatural freak burst into thousands of bloody, hairy, disgusting pieces that covered both Keira and me.

I may or may not have shrieked like a mating red fox as I tried to scoot away from the lion-guts rain while Keira exclaimed something like, "Ew! Gavyn, *what the hell?*" I couldn't really tell over the shrieking, which I'm not saying came from me but was definitely coming from *somewhere*.

Agnes pulled me to my feet, pointed toward Joachim and Nuada, who were battling an equally Nemean-esque beast, and yelled, "Go blow that one up, too!"

"I'm not a lion detonator!" I yelled back.

Agnes gestured angrily at the gooey mess all around us and snapped, "Then what do you call this?"

Okay, she had me there, but I had no clue how I'd even blown up that lion in the first place, and Havard was being characteristically silent about the whole thing, like he was forbidden from helping me in life-threatening situations.

But Keira pushed me toward Nuada and Joachim, and I attempted to cause a second lion explosion but only managed to hurt my wrist as the blade *literally* bounced off its equally steely mane. It wasn't until the lion swiped one of its plate-sized paws at Joachim, ripping open his sleeve and leaving long, bloody gashes in the fabric, that I realized my sword was glowing brighter again. It wasn't reacting to dangerous situations but to *me*. When my anxiety and fear and desire to protect those I cared about spiked, so did the sword's power.

I mimicked Keira and gripped the hilt in both hands, plunging it into the lion's back, and immediately turning my face away as the power within the sword caused a second massive feline explosion.

"This is so gross," Yngvarr muttered, shaking lion parts off his shoes and scraping some hairy bits from his pants with the tip of his sword.

I shrugged and said, "Yeah, but it's working."

The rest of the pride had backed off, forming a circle around us and prowling like they were actually considering how to tackle us now. I counted five of them, and only two were injured by the onslaught of arrows and swords from my allies. With the momentary breathing room, I thought back to every memory in which Havard used this sword, trying to piece together how I could use its power now to protect my friends and fill Sumer III's streets with their blood.

The image that popped into my head—as if being forced there—was of my grandfather, and his silver hair and lined face quickly dissolved into that of a young child with wide, terrified eyes as Keira took his hand and led him from the kitchen of his home. Havard had destroyed the entire house with one swipe of his sword.

"Okay, old man," I ordered. *"Wake your ass up and tell me how I can use the sword without hurting my friends."*

"You can't," he answered. *"It won't harm you because it's your power the sword draws on, but the only way to use it now is if one of the gods can protect everyone."*

I grunted in frustration, which earned me a few impatient glares, but continued my silent conversation. *"Like a force field?"*

I could almost sense Havard shrugging at me. *"Something like that."*

"God, you're annoying," I mumbled.

"I really hope that was directed at my brother," Yngvarr said. "Because now's not the time to alienate those trying to keep you alive."

"Of course I mean your brother," I retorted. "Now that you remember him, you *know* he's annoying as hell."

Yngvarr snickered and shrugged at me, too. "Runs in the family."

Havard laughed, so I mentally flipped him off before turning my attention back to the pacing lions whose low, throaty growls warned they were moments away from launching another attack.

Freyja slipped one of her swords back into the sheath crossing her back and said, "There's only one way to fight magic."

I pointed my sword at one particularly brutish lion and said, "Those are lions. Really, Freyja, you should visit a zoo sometime."

She didn't even roll her eyes at me and wisely chose to

ignore me instead. "I can't undo Ninhursag's spells, but I *can* cast some of my own here. Open your free hands."

We complied and lanterns immediately filled our grasps, their beams so unnaturally bright that even in the daytime, we couldn't stare at the lights without risking blindness. "Move them," Freyja ordered. "Flashing lights will generally scare off lions." She glanced at me and added, "And I didn't learn that in a *zoo*."

I waved my lantern around and said, "Discovery Channel. Zoo. What's the difference?"

This time, she *did* roll her eyes at me, but something else began happening, too. The lions' eyes had taken on feral looks, like the moving lights were far more terrifying than a bunch of gods and heroes with arrows and swords. And they were backing off, breaking their circle where'd they'd been methodically pacing, just trying to piece together how they could attack us without getting blown up.

But the lions, retreating into the nearest alleyway, were the first to get swept away by a new threat, one against which our weapons would be more useless than they'd been against the giant lions.

Because the alleyway had filled with a raging river far deadlier than the one that had nearly drowned us all in Sumer II.

We were standing at the delta of a river of blood.

CHAPTER FIFTEEN

Really, a river of blood was bad enough, but it quickly became clear this river was nothing like the tidal wave that almost drowned us in Sumer II. *Something* was moving in it, causing strange bulges and ripples. And the only thing worse than having to outrun a bloody river was imagining what could possibly be *living* in a bloody river.

One of the Valkyries screamed as a powerful red tide swept her away, and whatever was swimming inside it dragged her under. Keira shouted her name and turned as if she were actually going back for her, but I grabbed her arm and kept running. She stumbled but regained her footing then kept pace with me. A loud splash behind us made me glance over my shoulder, and I glimpsed a broad tail with a horizontal fin, just like a dolphin, but *this* fin had scales.

Agnes had glanced back, too, so as we ran, I yelled, "What in Sumer III *is* that thing?" I figured *the* Hell couldn't be any worse, so I might as well invoke one of the many hells I'd been to lately.

"I don't think you want to know," she yelled back.

Joachim used his bow to point toward a ziggurat on our

right, and we all changed course, heading toward the temple that would hopefully provide us with enough elevation to escape the flood. Adrenaline kept me from collapsing somewhere around the sixtieth step, but as soon as we reached the top—and, honestly, I lost count of the steps after one hundred—I dropped to the floor and put my head between my knees.

All around me, the Valkyries and gods did the same, panting and murmuring obscenities at Ninhursag and the bloody mess surrounding us and whatever was swimming in there, waiting for us to be stupid enough to jump in. Once I could breathe again, I nudged Agnes with my foot and demanded, "Okay, witch. What's in there and how do we kill it?"

She grunted at me but didn't lift her head.

So I grunted back at her and turned to Yngvarr. "Make her tell me."

"How?" he asked.

"I don't know. Threaten to withhold sex or something."

Yngvarr blinked at me then said, "I don't think it works that way. I don't think it's *ever* worked that way in the history of all things male and female."

Agnes sighed and finally lifted her head. "They're the kulullû, Gavyn."

"Why would you say that like I'd know what it is?" I asked.

I didn't know, obviously, but Havard did. "*Um... they're basically mermen.*"

"You have *got* to be kidding me," I snapped aloud.

Several Valkyries shot me annoyed glares, but come on... *mermen*? I had to fight King Triton now?

But the leaping merman that breached the surface of the bloody ocean surrounding us looked nothing like the pop culture images of mer-people. His torso and head were humanoid enough to recognize as vaguely human, but his eyes were bulging and too large for his face, his ears completely flat, his mouth lipless and tight. Gills ran the length of his neck, and his hands were webbed to form paddles. But worst of all, the creature either smiled or snarled at us, revealing a mouth filled with rows of pointed teeth, just like a shark's.

It would be impossible to romanticize *this* monstrosity.

The sea that had formed from the gushing river was steadily rising, meaning that our haven wouldn't be safe for long. He couldn't yet reach us, but I backed away from the edge of the temple floor anyway. Loud splashes alerted us about the arrival of our merman's reinforcements. We'd soon have them on every side.

"I'm sure you already know this," I said, "but being eaten by a merman is also a completely unacceptable way to die."

Keira actually nodded rather than scolding me.

"Any chance our flying horses can come rescue us?" I asked.

One of the Valkyries pointed to the sky and reminded me, "Force field. Nothing's getting through that Ninhursag doesn't want in here."

"Right," I sighed.

"So if we can't fly out, and we can't swim in demonic mermen infested blood, how do we actually get out of this?" Yngvarr asked.

We all looked to Freyja, hoping she had some more magic up her sleeves to save us from a hopeless situation. When she shrugged and admitted she was as clueless as the rest of us, I blurted out the first thing that popped into my head. "What about a boat?"

Fifty pairs of eyes slowly fell on me, all of them begging me never to speak again, but they should've known *that* was never going to happen.

"A boat," Keira repeated.

"Well, yeah. If we can float atop the bloody ocean, we can fight the mermen as they come near us. As soon as Ninhursag realizes we've found a way around this trap, she'll drain the blood and throw something else at us."

"But what's to stop the mermen from just tipping the boats over? And that's assuming Freyja can even use her magic to make boats in the first place," Joachim said.

"Make them really wide and flat," I suggested. "The more surface area, the more difficult it will be to tip. And heavy. Basically, just make us a bunch of houseboats."

"That's," Agnes snapped then crossed her arms as she squinted at me, "not the dumbest idea I've ever heard." She lifted her chin in the air and added, "But it's close."

Freyja tapped her chin with a finger as she thought, and for a few seconds, I had a reprieve from all those incredulous stares as they waited for Freyja to respond. Finally, she shrugged at me again and said, "I can create the boats. Doesn't mean your plan will actually work, but since this sea is still rising and we're running out of time, I'm not sure we have a choice."

Even though I should've known better by that point, I *still* expected to see some magic wand or sparkly lights or *something* to indicate a magical experience was about to occur, but Freyja simply uttered a few words and the first barge-like boat appeared at the edge of the ziggurat. I eyed it suspiciously and tapped my foot against it to ensure it was solid and I wouldn't just fall through it, which earned me a few eye rolls from several different gods, including Freyja, whom I appeared to be extraordinarily good at annoying. And I'm not gonna lie: I kinda got a kick out of how easily I could annoy her.

Frey passed me and stepped onto the boat, not even hesitating like he just boarded magical boats all the time. I was about to make a smartass comment about it, but Havard *finally* decided to be useful and stopped me before I could embarrass myself. "*He does have a magical ship, Gavyn. He owns Skidbladnir, the fastest ship in our world, which he can hide by folding it like a piece of paper and slipping it into his pocket.*"

"Dude," I exclaimed aloud, "*what?*"

Quite a few heavy sighs answered me, but I ignored them and glared at Frey. "If you've been carrying a fast, magic ship in your pocket this whole time, I *will* kick your ass."

Frey sighed heavily at me, too. "I don't have it with me, Gavyn."

"Well, don't you think that's the kind of thing you *should* carry around with you in case of emergencies like this?" I retorted. "You gods have a dozen weapons in your secret, hidden caches, but you wouldn't think to toss in a tiny magical *boat?*"

"Would you shut up and let me concentrate?" Freyja snapped.

If the bloody sea hadn't reached the top of the ziggurat where we were all standing, I wouldn't have shut up, because it seemed like a tremendous oversight to go into battle without every magical tool at our disposal... especially when they knew that battle was on an *island* and Frey had a magical boat he could have carried in his *pocket* if there was no room left in his weapons cache. But even Havard was begging me to shut up because my mental tirade was distracting him from Freyja's incantations, and I hadn't even noticed the second boat appear.

"I think we can all fit on three," she said. "Everyone start boarding."

A webbed hand suddenly broke the surface of the sea and grabbed Heidi's foot, who'd been about to board Frey's boat. I didn't know much about the Valkyries, other than their function to recover souls of slain warriors, but when she neither panicked nor screamed as that paddle-like appendage wrapped around her ankle, I was more than a little awed. I mean, I probably would've kept my cool, too, and not screamed like a banshee heralding *all* of our deaths but still.

With one swift, clean motion, her sword dropped to her side, separating the merman from his hand, then she kicked the now lifeless paddle away and stepped onto the boat. The merman, however, *did* shriek like a banshee heralding our deaths and by the number of ripples forming atop the sea, we could assume they were all kinda pissed off about having one of their buddy's hands cut off.

"Um... we should probably hurry," I said.

Keira pushed me toward the second boat where Agnes and Yngvarr waited as the rising flood allowed the mermen to pull themselves onto the top of the ziggurat and grasp wildly at legs as my allies attempted to board. Ull and Joachim, who hadn't boarded yet, fired arrows at the grotesque heads that kept popping out of the sea, but an impossibly huge number of these kulullû had arrived, all baring those rows of shark teeth and snapping at any body part close enough for it to reach.

Agnes produced her bow and quiver with her own witchy magic to help deter the mermen from getting too close, but I kept losing count of just how many sea monsters had surrounded us. And as I stared at all those mermen piling around us, the first flaw in my plan became obvious.

"So..." I said. "How do we actually *move* these barges? Think Freyja can make tugboats, too?"

Agnes shook her head and mumbled, "I knew we shouldn't let you make any plans."

"Hey," Keira said, "without Gavyn's idea, we'd all be piranha food right now, so lay off him."

I would've been a little more surprised by her defense of me if I hadn't been so busy stabbing a particularly nasty merman through his particularly nasty head.

"We can think through this," Yngvarr claimed. "The sea can only rise so much before it breaches the walls, and the last thing Ninhursag wants now is to let us all out of her cursed city. Not without the sword and Gavyn's life anyway."

"Thanks, buddy," I interjected.

"You're welcome," he said.

Smartass.

"*Family trait,*" Havard reminded me.

But Yngvarr continued thinking aloud before I could remind Havard of all the kinds of asses *he* was. "So the flood will stop soon, and as long as we stay toward the center of the barges and out of their reach, they won't be able to get to us. It would be suicide to try to crawl up here."

"Yeah, but all Ninhursag has to do is outwait us," I argued. "She's surrounded us with a bloody ocean and vicious sea monsters, and none of us thought to pack water and food. And I'm pretty sure even gods can die from dehydration."

"So we need to be able to move these boats," Agnes said.

I nodded and shouted at Freyja, "Hey, you forgot the outboard motors!"

She yelled back some colorful phrases that would transform this story's content rating, which I interpreted as, "We'll have to find some other way to move these boats."

It was Cadros, of all gods, who figured out a solution. I mean, he'd never struck me as the brightest of gods, but then again, pot and kettle and all that.

"We only have to reach the closest buildings," he said. "The streets are narrow enough that those of us with spears can use them to push off the sides of the building. One on each side of the boat, and it'll propel us forward."

I *couldn't* be shown up by a god I kept forgetting *existed*, so I crossed my arms and defiantly called back, "And how do you propose we *get* to those buildings?"

He grinned at me, produced a long spear from its mystical

hiding place, and twisted on one heel to face the bloody sea behind him. The whole thing was over before I could even piece together just what the hell—I mean, Sumer III—this guy was doing, but when I heard the shrieking and splashing and realized how he expected us to get to the street, I grimaced and murmured, "What is *wrong* with that guy?"

The mermen at the end of his spear continued to thrash wildly, and his cohorts swarmed around him, beating and pushing against the barge. And I reluctantly had to admit his plan *could* work, but using a speared fish-man as a propeller was just every kind of wrong. Sure, we were killing them as they attacked us, but these mermen weren't speared to death... just enough to keep them on the end like a harpoon.

I glanced at Keira and whispered, "This is ninety shades of wrong."

"It *is* cruel, but we don't really have a choice, Gavyn," she whispered back. Yngvarr had already followed suit, and our own fish on a hook was flailing around so much, we didn't need his friends to come to his aid and beat against our boat in order for it to move. But they came anyway, and as I watched the merman's dark blue-gray blood mix with the bright red, I realized one speared merman would never get us to our destination. The others had figured out how to pull the kulullû off the spears, but they weren't concerned about the injured fish-men.

They were only trying to stop our progress.

As soon as one merman was freed, another was speared, and the process repeated as we moved at what *seemed* like an agonizingly slow pace toward the street between the buildings. But Keira tore my attention away from the gruesome method of locomotion and pointed to the side of one of the skyscrapers.

"The sea-level is falling," she said. "Ninhursag is already draining it, getting ready to launch a different attack."

I sighed, expecting this would happen, of course, but dreading what might come next.

She didn't keep me waiting long.

From the center of the city, I could hear their barks and growls followed by the hissing of my name.

Of course she would have brought them back for my last showdown with her family, this one freakish hybrid I feared the most.

The devil dogs had returned.

CHAPTER SIXTEEN

The flood drained *preternaturally* quickly after I heard the hellhounds approaching from what I assumed was the only dry part of Sumer III. Either that, or they were excellent swimmers through thick, bloody seas. Cadros yanked his spear from one of the mermen, who flopped onto a sticky patch of ground, and after several awkward twitches and rolls, he lay still, presumably dead. How they'd breathed in an ocean of blood in the first place would most likely remain a mystery to me forever.

Freyja's barges landed in front of the buildings we'd been trying to get to, but I was reluctant to get off. I knew what was waiting for me at the end of this street. As if hearing my thoughts, hisses of "Gavyn" and "Die" and "Eat" echoed between the buildings, only this time, they'd added a new word to their vocabulary.

Sword.

So, naturally, I tried to hand the Sword of Asgard to Agnes, but she refused to take it from me. Yngvarr glanced in my direction and warned, "Don't even think about it," before I could try to pass it to him.

"So," Keira said. "These must be the infamous devil dogs."

"It gets better," I told her. "Wait until you *see* them."

Even Agnes flinched at the memory of their grotesque, vaguely human faces. Granted, we'd fought quite a few monsters that at least somewhat resembled humans, but there was something uniquely disturbing about the devil dogs' features and ability to speak, even if it were only in short, hissing bursts.

Ull nudged me with his bow to get me moving, but instead of walking into the street, I spun around and grabbed his bow from his hands then told everyone I was going home. Ull grabbed his bow back from me and said, "I don't touch your sword. You don't touch my bow."

"Dude, you are *such* a perv," I retorted.

"Get off the barge, Gavyn," Agnes ordered.

A memory of Tyr's laughter that usually erupted in moments like these sucker-punched me, and I had to close my eyes and take a few deep breaths to collect myself. I couldn't look weak in front of the Valkyries, after all. I'd be spending an eternity in their world soon, so I might as well vie for the title of most badass dead hero there, even though I *still* thought if we were all such badasses, we wouldn't have died in the first place.

"*Showing pain is a sign of weakness?*" Havard asked.

"*Shut up,*" I sighed.

"*Everyone misses him. Acknowledging your grief doesn't make you weak. It makes you normal,*" he persisted, so I tried telling him to shut up out loud, just in case he was having a hard time hearing me in my own head.

I expected those aggravated sighs that usually accompanied my conversations with Havard, so when they didn't come, I opened my eyes to see why. Keira and I were alone on the barge, the rest of our group having already entered the street between the buildings.

"I won't leave your side, Gavyn," she promised. "No matter what."

I swallowed even though my mouth was dry and brushed a few strands of her blond hair off her cheek. "I think maybe you were the one who was cursed most of all to fall in love with a guy like me."

She put her hand over mine and offered me a mischievous smile. "Maybe. But I think I can live with this curse."

I laughed and Yngvarr turned briefly to wave us on, but I *had* to tell her one more thing before entering the heart of Ninurta's city. "Keira, don't risk your life for me. You and I... we'll be together in Valhalla. But if you die—"

"Gavyn," she interrupted, "if you can't defeat Odin, he'll never forgive me for my past betrayals, and he'll never forgive you and your family for yours. Asgard will descend into the war Havard always feared. And neither of us will have a world left." She looked at the retreating backs of her sisters and my great-uncle, these people we cared about so deeply and added, "None of us will."

"It was only supposed to be the Sumerians," I argued. "You kidnapped me because I had to fight *them* and now—"

"How can you blame me for something I couldn't remember? I'm telling you *now* that you're far more important than me."

I backed away from her and demanded, "Don't ever say that again. *Nothing* is more important to me than you, and without you, there isn't a damn thing left worth fighting for."

I stepped off the barge and caught up to the rest of group trudging through the slippery street toward the city's center. I heard Keira following behind me, but she didn't try to get my attention or argue with me or tell me I couldn't be so selfish, not with so many other lives on the line. Maybe she knew it would be pointless, that I could never allow her to get hurt. Havard would have done anything to protect Arnbjorg; he would've destroyed any number of worlds and gods and mortals if he had to. How could anyone expect less of me?

With so many bodies in front of me, I couldn't really see what we were about to walk into. I could still *hear* the hissing and barking of the hellhounds but no one had starting screaming or cursing yet, so I assumed they hadn't reached us. But after a while, my legs began to ache, so obviously, I began to complain. "How long *is* this street?"

Keira lifted a shoulder then slowed her pace. "We *have* been walking a while, haven't we?"

"Sure as Sumer III seems like it," I mumbled, but it was also getting really hot, so I just assumed it was the combination of heat, knowing what lay ahead, and my own naturally sunny disposition.

But when Agnes slowed down as well and agreed we *had* walked farther than we should have given the length of the buildings and street, I groaned and complained one more time. "It's just like Sumer II. We may not be walking in the right direction even."

Everyone stopped as we considered our options, which were few. We could continue walking forward indefinitely, attempt to go back, even though we had no reason to believe there would be an end to the street that way either, or we could just stand around and hope Ninhursag would get bored enough to throw some new curveball at us. Personally, I voted for option three, but since I was the *only* one voting for standing around, I clearly lost the election.

"We've been in similar situations before," Agnes pointed out. "She's interfering with our senses, so we just need to figure out which way is northwest since I'm pretty sure we landed on the southeast side of the island and have been traveling inward toward the center since we walked through the gate."

"I'm not a Boy Scout," I retorted. "I don't carry a compass with me everywhere I go."

"We probably *should*," Yngvarr supplied helpfully.

"*And* a foldable magic boat," Keira also supplied helpfully.

"And water," I added just as helpfully. "And a can of beans."

"Beans?" Keira repeated. "Why beans?"

I shrugged and replied, "Isn't that what Boy Scouts eat on camping trips?"

"I can't believe I once thought you were so hot," Róta said.

"I get that a lot," I agreed.

Ull squinted at the sun then sighed angrily. "That's no help. Not the real sun."

"How can you tell?" I asked.

"Color and size are all wrong."

I squinted at the sun, too, but it just looked like the sun to me. "Are you a sun god now?"

But mentioning sun gods just reminded me of Ra and how easily any of us could die, so I waved him off before he could answer. "Doesn't matter. If the sun can't direct us, how can we figure out which way is north?"

"Anybody have a magnet?" Keira asked.

"That's really more practical than carrying around a compass?" I asked back.

"Um," Joachim said, "I have an idea. We have plenty of knives, so as long as some of you have hammers or mallets stashed in your secret hiding places, we can experiment trying to find north by laying the iron blades in different directions and striking them until one becomes magnetized. Once it does, we'll know that direction is north."

I blinked at him as I waited for that, "Ha! Can't believe you fell for that," moment, but he just arched an eyebrow at me and reminded me, "Electrical engineer. And I've done this before. It *will* work."

So even though I knew he was way smarter than me, I still looked at Keira as if I expected her to agree with me that our German hero was out of his mind. Instead, she just nodded along as if she should've thought of that first, except she actually *was* smart enough to have thought of that first.

But Joachim's idea didn't require me to walk aimlessly down a magical street that wouldn't end, so I figured I might as well play along and pulled out the only knife I had, an old iron blade that I separated from its hilt with the mallet Cadros handed me. After the whole spearing mermen thing, I was kinda afraid to ask him what other weapons he had stored in his secret cache. Of course, that didn't stop me and I asked anyway.

Cadros snickered, which was as close to a laugh as I'd ever get from him, and said, "All sorts of things. You never know what you'll need in battle."

"Then why don't you have a compass?" I asked.

"A compass isn't a weapon," he said so matter-of-factly that I actually felt stupid for pointing out the flaw in his always-be-preparedness.

I picked a direction I thought might be north, and Keira stepped on the opposite end of the blade to keep it still as I began to beat on it with my mallet. I'd occasionally pause to see if the sliver of iron Ull had broken off an arrowhead with his bare hands would stick to the blade I was beating the shit out of, but not surprisingly, it never worked.

I was about to tell Joachim he needed to get reimbursed for his degrees when Agnes shouted, "Got it." She stood up and pointed to the side of the building. "That's north, which is slightly off from geographical north, so I think we need to go a bit to the left to be heading northeast again."

"And for those of us who aren't witches and can't walk through brick walls?" I asked.

"Illusions, Gavyn," Agnes said. "The road actually turns and it only *looks* like a solid wall, but there's a section we'll all be able to walk through."

The devil dogs hissed "Gavyn" and "sword" to agree with her, and to my horror, I realized she was right. We could all hear the hellhounds so well because they were on the opposite side of the fake portion of the wall, just waiting for us to cross.

My sword grew brighter with the knowledge I would soon be facing my mortal enemies—not the Sumerians but those damn dogs—and I thought about just staying on the ground while everyone else walked through this magic portal. But Keira would be one of those facing the hellhounds soon, so I let her pull me to my feet and we began probing the wall for the fake section.

And because my luck usually worked out this way, I was the one to find it, which meant everyone expected me to go in first. I pulled my hand back and shot Keira my best, "Please don't make me go in there," look but Agnes was already pushing me through. And, of course, Keira was right beside me, with my great-uncle and own personal witch close behind.

The red, sticky tiles we'd been walking on immediately transformed to a pristine blue, but I had little time to appreciate how bloodless and clean this part of Sumer III was. The hard ticking of sharp nails hitting those turquoise tiles mixed with the barking and hissing of my biggest fan club.

"Die," one said.

"Eat," said another.

"Go back to Hell!" said I.

I caught Keira's sickened expression just as the closest devil dog leapt toward me, catching the tip of my sword beneath his front left leg. He yelped as I stepped aside, and he landed on the no longer pristine tiles since drops of his blood now formed bright red polka dots against the turquoise blue.

Ninhursag must've anticipated a far larger force than we'd amassed before, because I'd never encountered so many hellhounds at once, not even in the tunnels of Sumer II. This pack was so large, they had to crawl over one another as they attempted to be the loyal canine that finally killed me and retrieved my coveted sword.

Arrows zipped past me, often finding their marks but rarely stopping those demonic beasts. The dog I'd injured sprang at me again while Keira stabbed another one trying to ambush me from behind. The whole time, my sword grew brighter and brighter, but I'd become so accustomed to fighting with a regular, unenchanted sword that I continued to slice and stab at the devil dogs as they continued to snarl and hiss my name.

After killing several of those damn hellhounds as an endless tide of them poured from some mystical, devil dog factory, Havard finally shouted, *"You have the gods' most powerful weapon in your hands—use it!"*

His voice and command startled me so much, one of those devil dogs almost latched onto my arm with his razor sharp teeth inside his sort-of human mouth. And I'm pretty sure that would've resulted in my immediate insanity and maybe even committing hara-kiri.

I managed to pivot and swing my sword back around to decapitate the devil dog and maybe it was just my imagination, but the blade seemed sharper, cutting easily through the normally tough hide and thick sinew and bone.

If I'd had time to practice using this sword's power, I would've known exactly what Havard wanted me to do now, but instead, I gutted another hellhound as he yelled at me again. *"Pull all of your anger and fear and hatred of these mutts into the sword and strike them down!"*

"What in Asgard is *that* supposed to mean?" I shouted back at him. This time, no one shot me any irritated scowls because they were all too busy trying not to die. Beside me, Cadros swung his blade at a devil dog leaping toward him, but the devil dog crouched beneath his sword then jumped, managing to get its knife-like teeth around Cadros's neck.

I shouted for Keira to cover me and spun around, hitting the dog with as much strength as I could muster, which turned out to be a veritable crap ton because the hellhound exploded, sending devil dog fragments all over the now slippery turquoise tiles.

Cadros collapsed as soon as the mutt disintegrated, and Agnes dropped to his side while Yngvarr protected her from the unceasing attacks. My whole body became numb as I watched her check Cadros for signs of life, but his neck was so mangled from the devil dog's teeth, I already knew her answer.

Agnes lifted her eyes to mine and shook her head, and something within me snapped, just like that day in the hotel room when I'd injured Frey, unable to control my own body. I didn't notice Keira or the others backing away from me, nor did I notice the Sword of Light changing once again. If I had, I would've known its normal yellow glow had deepened to a brilliant, shimmering orange. I would've noticed Freyja murmuring another spell, which I would've later learned was her own sort of force field to protect our allies. But the only thing I noticed were the faces of those hellhounds who'd taken the life of a god trying to protect my world.

My arms swung wildly like a hitter at bat, and each time the Sword of Light touched one of the devil dogs, it turned to ash and the dark gray flakes floated in angry tornadoes all around me. Soon, I was walking through a storm cloud of ash, hardly able to see, but I kept slashing at every growl and whimper and scared hissing of my name and threats of my death.

When Sumer III seemed too quiet, I still marched through the inches of ash, leaving footprints of destruction in my wake, as I searched for more hellhounds to incinerate. But the city had become eerily quiet, at least until I heard her calling my name.

"Gavyn, they're gone. They're all gone."

I stopped marching and listened.

"Gavyn..." Footsteps behind me.

"Keira, don't," another voice warned.

"It's okay. He'd never hurt me."

A hand on my shoulder. I flinched, but she was right. I could never hurt her.

I slowly turned and she touched my face, and I remembered who and where I was. So I lowered my sword and its light dimmed, returning to its pale yellow glow, and with my free hand, I traced my thumb over a small cut on her cheek. "Too many of us are going to die," I whispered.

"Yes," she agreed. "But we're soldiers, Gavyn. We all know the cost of war."

I let out a slow breath and vowed, "Not again. When this is all over, gods everywhere will fear us heroes. I'll send them a message they can never forget: threaten our world again, and we'll destroy every last one of you."

CHAPTER SEVENTEEN

As we crossed through the ashy streets of Sumer III, heading toward the city's center where we suspected Ninurta and his horde of gods and demigods awaited us, I caught up to Agnes and Nuada and walked beside them for a while, unable to articulate what I *wanted* to say but couldn't figure out how. It finally came out in a single word, which conveyed everything yet nothing. "Sorry."

When Agnes glanced at me, she seemed startled. "For what?"

"For Cadros."

"Gavyn, you didn't kill him. You tried to save his life."

I shook my head, because I felt responsible for his death anyway. So many of these gods and heroes and Valkyries pooled around me, believing they needed to protect me more than others, and I knew that was exactly why Cadros had been fighting so closely to me. "I was so focused on keeping those hellhounds away from Keira... if I'd been paying more attention—"

"Gavyn," Nuada interrupted. "Cadros died an honorable death. A war god's death. That's the best he could hope for."

For some reason, hearing he died some honorable death, whatever *that* was supposed to mean, just pissed me off, so I stopped in the street, causing Heidi to bump into me and mumble an awkward apology. But the whole concept of honorable deaths was ridiculous, some machismo on steroids, out of control bravado that allowed us to excuse the murder of other people. This wasn't the kind of world I wanted to live in, yet I'd be *forced* into Valhalla soon. I'd be trained to fight in some mythical battle that may or may not ever happen and for *what*? Maybe I didn't understand the whole concept of Ragnarok, but I understood *my* world and I refused to believe it could never change. If I accepted that, I might as well really quit and go home.

In that intuitive way of hers, Agnes sensed what was troubling me and urged Nuada on while she stood with me in the street, staring into my eyes the whole time, which made me more than a little uncomfortable so I said, "Don't get any ideas. Yngvarr's right over there, and Keira gets crazy jealous."

But Agnes didn't even make a smartass comment in reply. She just kept staring at me and when the rest of our party had passed us, she said, "Peace is the greatest illusion of them all. It's the greatest myth man has ever told. You have to let go of this idea that we can change the world, Gavyn."

I caught my breath as a memory of my mother, placing her frail hands on my shoulders, reminded me that I once held such certainty in this greatest myth and that I could play a part in bringing it to life. My mother had smiled, looked me in the eyes, and said, "Gavyn, one day you're going to change the world."

And I'd believed her because I was a child, and as children, we believe the lies our parents tell us.

I held up my sword, this artifact of my past, and believed her because as an adult, I believed in hope and love and justice and possibilities. So I met Agnes's gaze again and told her, "Yes, I can change the world. And I'm going to."

I wove through bodies to catch up to Keira and took a deep breath as the glow of my sword alerted me that we were getting close to the Sumerians who were awaiting us. "I love you, Keira," I said. "Despite everything that's happened and everything that will, I'm glad you came for me because I wouldn't change knowing you for anything."

"Gavyn," she replied, but if she was about to pour her heart out to me one last time, a screeching dragon cut her off, one filled with poison, which made it impossible to kill. Tiamat had been brought to Sumer III.

We'd reached the city's center, a courtyard surrounded by those colossal skyscrapers, and a single fountain that bubbled what I *hoped* was water. The turquoise tiles gave way to sand-colored bricks, but unlike Marduk's Babylon, there was no vegetation here, no awnings or coverings or even doors to the buildings so we could hide from the dragon.

We were completely exposed as we prepared for what I assumed would be an excruciatingly painful death. And if Keira *had* to die, I wasn't going to let it be like this. "Get against the side of the buildings!" I shouted as I climbed onto the fountain, careful not to touch whatever flowed through it. All of my friends and allies argued with me, wanting to follow me or talk me out of whatever crazy scheme I was concocting now, but since I really only had half an idea, and it was a pretty stupid one at that, I again ordered them to get against the wall, just in case my Hail Mary didn't work.

"Hey, you bitch!" I yelled at Tiamat, which she didn't seem to appreciate. I mean, that was kinda the whole point, but I'm not gonna lie: I cringed a bit and had some serious reservations about my half-cocked, suicidal plan as she screeched and flapped her wings to dive toward me.

This time, I knew the blade of the Sword of Light had

deepened to that fiery orange, and I gripped the hilt in one hand as I waited as still as I could, but really, I just wanted to jump down from the fountain and find my flying horse to get me off this gods-forsaken island. Her mouth opened and I pulled Odin's shield off my back just as the stream of fire, which could have been poisonous fire, for all I knew, hit the enchanted wood and formed a blazing wall in front of me. As soon as Tiamat stopped trying to flame roast me, I dropped the shield and jumped toward her, stabbing the tip of my sword into her scaled stomach.

The sound of her screaming combined with the screams of my friends below, who must've thought I'd lost my mind, what little there was to lose, by intentionally piercing a poison-filled dragon's body. But I'd reasoned, which, in hindsight, was an incredibly dangerous thing for me to do, that the poison would be some kind of liquid and didn't liquids evaporate with enough heat?

I found myself belatedly wishing I'd paid more attention in chemistry.

Tiamat's screaming vanished, and I fell to the ground with a slightly painful tweak of an ankle. I covered my head, like that would do any good if poisonous rain was about to fall on me, but the only thing that covered me was the same kind of dark gray ash my sword had caused when killing the devil dogs.

Keira fell at my side and pulled on my arm, urging me to hurry to my feet, and my initial thought was that Tiamat was either resurrecting herself *or* the fountain had turned to some kind of acid after all. But what I saw was far worse.

We'd been surrounded, as if the horde of Sumerian gods and demigods had materialized out of thin air. And if I had arrived on Grande Terre with a squadron of warriors, Ninurta had amassed a battalion.

"Oh, this isn't good," I muttered.

Keira shook her head as my allies grouped closer to me like I would somehow magically know how to get us out of this predicament. But really, there was only one way out and it was the sole reason we'd come here, the one thing we'd been preparing for since a group of Sumerian gods stood on a ziggurat and televised their arrival to the world.

We'd have to fight. And I'd have to face Ninurta, even if it killed us both.

Freyja's face darkened as a particular goddess caught her attention and she hissed, "Inanna's mine."

So, naturally, I assumed there was a story there and wanted to know what that whole rivalry and hatred was about, but when I tried to ask, she looked at me like I'd grown a second head and snapped, "Do you really think we have time for this *now*?"

I shrugged and said, "Nobody's doing anything, so why not?"

Even Havard sighed irritably in my mind, and it was obvious Freyja had no intention of telling me why she hated Inanna, so I scanned the Sumerian battalion until I found Ninhursag and Enki and flipped them off. Agnes scolded me, Yngvarr muttered something about how could we *possibly* be related, and Keira just pointed out the obvious. "I don't see Marduk. He's either hiding so he can swoop in if the battle turns against his family, or he's not here."

"And if he's not here, why?" I asked.

Ninhursag must've had some kind of bat hearing because she answered my question, even though she should've been out of earshot. "Because Marduk refused to join us."

And since *we* should've been out of earshot yet we heard every word she spoke, we all realized there were no secrets in Sumer III and every word we uttered aloud would be fodder for our enemies. There'd be no strategizing, no planning a way out of this fight.

"You helped us kill your own heroes," I shouted back, even though shouting was clearly unnecessary. I just wanted to yell at her for betraying us and forcing me to fight all those devil dogs.

Ninhursag shrugged as if those lives were irrelevant. After all, they were just demigods.

I turned my attention back to Ninurta, whose eyes were still fixed on the sword in my hands. I slipped the shield off my shoulder again and held it ready for combat, and the Sumerian god of war lifted his gaze to meet mine. And that bastard actually *smiled* at me, like he was confident in his victory and knew he'd soon control both the Sword of Asgard and Earth.

Yngvarr let out a quick, angry breath, and he murmured, "Zababa. I've waited thirty years to avenge my brother's death."

And Zababa actually smiled at *him*, like murdering my great-grandfather had been the highlight of his long, evil life. Really, there was a lot of smiling going on, but in that creepy, homicidal lunatics kind of way rather than the, "Hey, we're so happy to see you!" normal person kind of way.

Ninurta finally stepped forward, separating himself from his battalion to offer what he thought was a final compromise, an act of mercy in his deranged mind. "You're outnumbered, Gavyn. Overpowered. We both know you can't possibly survive here. Put down the sword and surrender, and I'll allow you all to leave."

I snickered and said, "Sounds like you're scared, Ninurta. If we're so overpowered, why would you let us walk away?" Of course, I already knew why he'd just let us walk away: if I gave up my sword, we'd never stand a chance against Odin, so Ninurta was banking on us dying either way.

He shrugged. "I'm feeling generous. I'm sure it won't last."

"You'd have to possess a soul to feel compassion or

generosity," I countered. "And any god who allows humans to sacrifice themselves for his gain has no soul."

"On the contrary," Ninurta replied. "Thanks to those sacrifices, I possess many souls."

"Okay," I decided. "I think our time for monologuing is up."

Apparently, my enemies and allies agreed with me, because all Hell broke loose. The Sumerian heroes charged us, some even shouting what I assumed was a battle cry, while Agnes and Yngvarr slipped through the melee to find the gods they'd already targeted. Ninurta, of course, was mine, had always been my cross to bear, the one god whose death was *my* responsibility. And he stood perfectly still at the edge of what had turned into the battlefield, waiting for me as if he'd been obsessed with this final battle, too. And maybe he had been. Maybe it had kept him up at night as well as he imagined my death and what victory would mean for him.

A demigod on my left attacked me, and I managed to get my shield up before his sword could slice off my arm. I pivoted on my heel and swung my blade low to his leg, but I held the Sword of Asgard in my hand. It didn't just cut the guy's leg, leaving a gaping wound and causing him to fall like a normal sword. It cut his leg *off*, and the poor bastard collapsed, screaming and clutching frantically at the stump near his hip. I quickly faced Ninurta again, but he seemed completely unconcerned about the power of my sword. He waited patiently, holding Sharur as if his own magical talking weapon could compete with the magic of the Sword of Light.

No other heroes or Sumerian gods dared to fight me as I approached Ninurta. I tried to keep track of those I'd grown closest to—Keira, of course, and Yngvarr, and even Agnes—but it became impossible as the swarm of bodies and sounds of metal hitting shields and the occasional cries of those wounded in battle filled the courtyard, turning the battlefield into one bloody, noisy, chaotic scene. I didn't even know if we were winning or losing or if it even mattered, because maybe, we were *all* destined to lose anyway.

Ninurta's attention briefly left me as his eyes flickered to my right, and I risked looking away from him to see why. Freyja and Inanna had been engaged in their own fight, but Freyja had dealt a painful blow to the Sumerian goddess, who'd fallen to her knees but still managed to keep her shield in front of her and her sword swinging at Freyja each time she advanced.

It was the only time Ninurta registered any emotion at all.

As his attention shifted back to me, he held Sharur to his lips and murmured, but either the noise of battle or Ninhursag's magic prevented me from hearing his command. His fingers loosened around the shaft of his spear, and it flew toward me, alarmingly fast and with perfect precision. I lifted my shield, but whatever Ninurta had been doing with those souls apparently worked, because Sharur actually penetrated the wood of my shield, but it didn't get stuck. Instead, it returned to Ninurta's hand so he could command it again.

"Dude," I shouted, "that's cheating!"

Okay, I had a magical weapon, too, but at least *my* magical weapon was staying in my hands. Granted, if my sword could fly, I'd probably try the same thing, but still.

Sharur flew toward me again, but since the tip of the spear had come within inches of my face, I decided Odin's stupid enchanted shield would be useless in my fight against Ninurta and tossed it to the ground. I thought I heard Keira yelling at me, and if she were, it was probably to call me a dumbass, but I couldn't depend on a shield to protect me. Sharur flew at me with that supernatural speed, but my demigod reflexes kicked into frantic mode, and I gripped my sword with both hands and knocked it aside. Instead of falling to the ground, it returned to Ninurta, and I used the brief interlude to run toward him, hoping to get in close range before Sharur could attack me again.

I'd just reached striking distance when Ninurta pulled a sword from his own secret hiding place and deflected my attack. He still held Sharur in his left hand and jabbed it toward my side. I was spared from impalement by the force of my sword being deflected and knocking his spear away from my body. In other words, I'd gotten extraordinarily lucky.

Somehow, the magic of my sword didn't seem to work on Ninurta. His sword didn't turn to ash nor did he. I retreated a few steps to regain my balance and quickly reassess how I could possibly kill a god far more powerful than me and far more powerful than the weapon I'd been led to believe could defeat him. But what if everyone had been wrong? What if the Sword of Light was useless against a ruthless god of war who viewed mortals as tools for his own empowerment? No, I refused to believe that. He *had* to have a weakness.

I advanced again, and he deflected this attack, too, this time with so much force I actually stumbled backwards and my stomach dropped as I realized I was completely outmatched. Ninurta didn't look concerned at all. I was simply a nuisance that stood in his way of total domination, and it was only a matter of time—and a short amount of time, at that—before no one would stand in his way of demanding the world's subjugation.

"*Havard, wake your ass up and help me here!*" I shouted.

I expected him to ignore me as usual, but he actually answered me. "*What is your weakness, Gavyn?*"

I immediately answered, "*Keira.*"

"*Yes,*" he agreed. "*Just as Arnbjorg was mine. And what did the Sword of Prophecy show you?*"

Inanna. It had shown me Inanna falling from the cliff rather than the man's body they'd sacrificed, because I'd shown up and slain her with my sword then pushed her body into the ocean. In the heat of battle, I'd forgotten her death was the key to defeating Ninurta.

Instead of advancing again, I spun around and ran toward Inanna, who would've been defeated by Freyja anyway, but I *had* to break Ninurta's focus. The Sumerian goddess was too busy protecting herself from Freyja's attacks to notice my approach, but Ninurta yelled her name and what I assumed was a warning, but I was too close and it was too late. I dropped to the ground behind her, never intending to kill her myself but assuming Ninurta would want to protect the goddess he loved by killing *me*.

And as I'd anticipated, Sharur narrowly missed me and impaled the Sumerian goddess in her back. Her arms stretched out to her sides, her sword dropping to the bricks with a clang that echoed through the courtyard, even through the clamor of the battle that didn't stop to mourn the death of this goddess who'd helped engineer the Sumerians' return to our world.

But I sensed a change in the air around me, a shifting of some immense force. I leapt to my feet, knowing Ninurta would set his sights on the only revenge that could possibly rival his pain, and the Sumerian god finally demonstrated his powers had never been limited to war. Dark clouds formed overhead and the sky exploded as thousands of lightning bolts streaked toward the ground, striking all around us in deafening blows. Electricity became a visible, tangible, *living* thing in the courtyard as Ninurta's rage burst from his body.

"*This was a* really *bad idea,*" I told Havard.

"*No,*" he argued. "*He has lost his ability to reason. He is only pain and anger now. This is your only chance to best him while Freyja is able to protect you, but her magic won't last long against him.*"

"*How am I supposed to* best *him?*" I cried. "*He's about to fry us all!*"

"Then you'd better hurry."

I mentally told Havard exactly what I thought he should do and where he should do it, but since we likely had minutes, if not seconds, to live, I charged Ninurta anyway. Sharur hadn't returned to his hand, presumably because he refused to fight with a weapon that was covered in Inanna's blood, but he still held the sword that had deflected my previous attacks. The Sword of Asgard had become pure light, and from its blade, streaks of orange and yellow and red burst forth just like Ninurta's lightning. As I swung the sword, Ninurta held his own sword vertically to attempt another deflection, but this time, my blade cut through his.

He pulled another sword from his cache and stepped back, trying to buy himself a few seconds so Freyja's magic would collapse under the weight of his own as the lightning continued to explode around us like fireworks. I assumed all of my allies were still fighting, but the sounds of battle had vanished. Maybe the lightning strikes *had* deafened me. Or maybe my world had narrowed to this moment and only Ninurta and I existed in it. I sliced and he blocked and lost another blade but pulled a third from its hiding place and continued to retreat as I continued to advance.

And then Ninurta's back hit a wall, and he was forced to confront me and all of my own rage and pain that would forever be colored with the faith my mother had held in me. Ninurta shook his head and hissed, "Impossible," like he couldn't fathom an outcome other than his victory, and certainly not a defeat at the hands of a demigod like me.

I swung my sword just as Freyja's magic broke and the battlefield erupted in sparks and fire and agonizing screams that didn't die away as the Sword of Asgard passed through Ninurta's body. The Sumerian god of war erupted just like Sumer III, and the sparks and fire that had comprised him drifted to the bloody ground.

And as I turned to find my friends, praying they were still alive, I realized *I* was still alive.

My prophecy, my fated death, had never been about Ninurta but the god who'd started it all, the god whose greed and lust for power had turned him against his own people.

And I knew I wasn't finished. I had to bring the Sword of Asgard home.

ODIN RETURNS TO ASGARD

(And Havard's Story Comes to an End. Finally.)

Asgard awoke to torrential rains on the last day of my life. In all of my centuries, in my long and storied life, I'd never seen rain like this in Asgard. Arnbjorg joined me at the window of our bedroom and pulled her quilt tighter around her shoulders as she watched the black sky with me, the flooding ponds forming across the palace grounds. Neither of us spoke for a long time, sensing the rains were a portent of what was coming but selfishly wanting just a little more time with one another despite the nearly seven hundred years we'd been blessed to share.

And I'd loved every moment of it, every memory as cherished as the next.

"How will it happen?" she finally asked.

"I don't know," I admitted.

A knock on the palace door startled us both and Geirr, our servant, appeared at our bedroom before either of us could finish dressing. I slipped into the hallway and he lowered his voice to tell me, "Tyr and Frey have arrived, my lord. Odin has returned and sits on his throne in Valaskjalf."

"He's returned alone?" I asked, although I already knew

the answer. Hadn't my sword warned me of this day for so long?

Geirr said he did not know and urged me to greet my guests, these gods who'd become champions of my rule. As we descended the stairs, I whispered, "Has Yngvarr returned?"

My brother, mercifully, had been in the Otherworld with Badb for the past month. If he were here, he'd almost certainly interfere with Fate's intentions, and how could that possibly work out in our favor?

Upon reaching the dining hall, Tyr recited a list of gods who'd sworn their allegiance to me and begged me to reconsider leading them into battle against Odin.

I put my hand on his shoulder and told him, "Old friend, if we lose Asgard, we've gained nothing."

"You don't know that Asgard will be destroyed," he insisted.

"We should go to his palace," Frey suggested. "Find out if war is inevitable before assuming it is."

"Always our voice of reason," I replied with a smile.

Frey smiled back at me, but it was as forced as mine. There was no joy that morning, no happiness to be found in our world. He shrugged and said, "It's in my nature, after all."

By now, Arnbjorg had finished dressing and joined us downstairs just as Frey was offering to make the trip to see Odin.

"Frey," she sighed. "That's suicide. Surely you understand Odin is beyond all hope of reconciliation."

Tyr scratched his chin with his good hand as he thought, occasionally thinking aloud, but none of us had answers to his questions. "Where has he been all this time? And what has he been doing? I was expecting an invasion, but there's no army in Asgard."

"Isn't there?" I asked. "Perhaps all he's been doing is waiting for us to tear ourselves apart."

Thunder rolled overhead just as someone else knocked on our door. We fell silent as Geirr allowed this third visitor inside, and as she stepped into the hall, she pushed the hood of her cloak off her head, water pooling at her feet. She caught Arnbjorg's gaze and said, "We need to talk."

No one—not even Astrid and Áki—knew what we'd asked Freyja to do for us. Now that this day had come, I realized what a burden we'd placed on her, to live all those years virtually alone in the knowledge of Asgard's truth. Arnbjorg nodded and followed the goddess from the hall while I attempted to persuade Tyr to calm his troops. But it soon became clear we'd have far less control of a civil war than we'd hoped.

Outside, the sounds of shouting and skirmishes combined with the relentless rain and thunder, and we dropped all conversation, all discussion of negotiations and attempts to broker peace as we ran from my palace to Valhalla's field where my supporters were already clashing with Odin's warriors.

The mud of the battlefield quickly mixed with the blood of the dead and wounded and I shouted for a truce, but each time I tried to end the fighting, the thunder drowned out my voice.

"Thor," I murmured. I grabbed Frey's arm and begged him to find the god of thunder so he could bring this storm to an end. Surely, he'd sympathize with wanting to save the lives of countless gods.

Frey immediately obeyed, leaving Tyr and me alone at the edge of the battlefield. "Seeing you may only make things worse," Tyr reasoned. "If you're set on pursuing a peaceful resolution, let me talk to both sides."

"Thank you, Tyr," I replied. And knowing I'd never see

him again, I quickly added, "You've always been a good friend and the most honorable god I've ever known."

I turned to leave just as Freyja and Arnbjorg reached us, and I jerked a thumb over my shoulder toward the slaughter behind me. "Do you think they'll listen to you?" I asked Freyja.

"Of course not," she said. "It was never a secret my brother and I allied with you. Surely, Havard, you're not so naïve as to believe there's any other resolution to this war than the one we've planned and prepared for."

"I'm not," I assured her.

Freyja glanced at Arnbjorg then lowered her face, touching my arm and taking Arnbjorg's hand. "I wish it didn't have to end this way."

I wiped the rain from my eyes and tried to express my gratitude for all she'd done for us and all she still had to do, but I heard Áki screaming my name, and all other concerns vanished. Arnbjorg's eyes grew round and she clutched her stomach as our son-in-law barreled into us, grasping desperately at my arms. "They've taken her. My lord, they've taken her!"

"Astrid," Arnbjorg breathed.

But Áki shook his head. "No. Hjordis. They've taken our daughter!"

The rain and thunder suddenly stopped then, either because Frey had found Thor and convinced him to change the weather or because it was the second omen ushering my wife and me to our deaths. There would be only one way to save my granddaughter's life.

"We'll find her, Áki," I promised. "And we'll get her back safely to you."

Of course, I had no idea where the mystery gods could've taken her, but this was the moment I'd known was coming for nearly a thousand years. And I didn't need the Sword of

Prophecy to tell me where to find my granddaughter. My heart already knew they'd come to me.

I took Arnbjorg's hand, and told Áki to protect Astrid and warn his sons not to engage in any of these battles. Áki nodded but hesitated then threw his arms around us both. "I've dreaded this day for so long," he cried. "I don't know how to say goodbye to you."

"You don't," I replied. "Arnbjorg and I won't really be gone. Only our bodies will die, but you'll see, Áki. We'll live on in your children and their children, and one day, all of our pain from this day will be avenged."

Our embrace broke, and Arnbjorg thanked him for loving our daughter and treating her so well then we left him to reach the gods who'd abducted Hjordis. I feared if we didn't encounter them soon, they'd grow impatient and harm her. Arnbjorg and I didn't speak as we rushed home, although I occasionally caught her stealing glimpses of Asgard as if trying to capture these last moments, final snapshots of the world where we'd been allowed to live so long and raise our family and watch our children raise their own.

A fire erupted near the wall surrounding our realm, and we slowed our pace as we estimated what was burning. "Heimdall's watch tower?" she guessed.

"Yes," I agreed. "Perhaps Odin's invasion is coming, after all."

We'd just reached the edge of our palace grounds when a second fire broke out closer to Valhalla.

Asgard was burning. And if we didn't end this war soon, there would be nothing left but ash.

Hjordis's voice stopped us both as she screamed, and the nameless god whose face I knew so well dragged her from our palace steps. She saw us and screamed again, begging us to leave, worried about *our* fates rather than her own, even though she'd known this day would come. That was the spirit she'd always possessed: brave and selfless and stronger than any god in any realm.

I held up my hands and called out to the god holding a knife to my granddaughter's throat. "I know what you want. Let her return home and you can have it."

The god, who was joined by a second one I didn't recognize, laughed, not believing I'd give up so easily.

"Please," I begged. "No sword is worth her life."

"But is she worth yours?" he asked.

"She is worth everything," I answered without hesitation.

The two unfamiliar gods glanced at each other and conferred in a language I didn't speak but could identify.

Sumerian.

Of course it would be the Sumerians, whose ties to my father had connected *me* to their pantheon as well. What deal had he struck with them so long ago when he'd stolen the Sword of Asgard from Odin and gave it to Inanna? And why had she returned it to me? But most worrisome now was the deal Odin had made, what he'd promised them in exchange for the sword and my life. Odin wanted an uncontested reign over Asgard, but what did the Sumerians want? And was it something I could risk allowing them to have?

I met Hjordis's eyes and immediately had my answer

"No deceptions," I assured the Sumerian gods. "I will lay down my sword, and neither my wife nor I will fight you as long as you let her go unharmed."

Any minute now, Yngvarr and Badb would return to Asgard. News of this sort traveled quickly among gods. And once Yngvarr arrived, it would be too late to save Hjordis, because he'd refuse to accept my sacrifice, and the Sumerians would take her life instead of mine.

"Come closer," the Sumerian god ordered, "and lay your sword at Dagan's feet. Once it is in his hands, I will let your granddaughter go. You have my word."

If I hadn't been granted this prophecy, I would've questioned his word and its worth, but this was exactly how my life was supposed to end and how a new life for my daughter and her children would begin. I placed the Sword of Asgard at Dagan's feet and backed away from him as he hurriedly grabbed it from the ground and the nameless god pushed Hjordis away from him, ordering her to run home, but she hesitated and wanted to run to us instead.

"Go," I told her. "You have your own destiny to fulfill."

Although she'd been grown for quite some time, she suddenly seemed so small now, like a child again as she shook her head and cried for us, but the Sumerian gods had no intention of belaying their own orders for our family's dramatic separation. Dagan handed the sword to the nameless god and pushed me to my knees, and Arnbjorg shouted at Hjordis, admonishing her for not leaving and telling her one last time to go and promising her she would never leave her. Dagan grabbed my wife's arm and forced her to kneel beside me.

I would never learn if Hjordis obeyed her grandmother, if she immediately left or if she witnessed the death of her grandparents.

I would also never know how much time passed between my death and seeing Asgard again but through different lenses, as if I were privy to multiple perspectives that showed me different parts of our world, and it should've been confusing, but somehow, it wasn't.

And so, I discovered the Sword of Asgard's fate and my children's, and somehow, I knew I had to be with them until Odin was dethroned and the rightful heir of Asgard took his place. Only one aspect of my life had ended, but in other ways, it had just begun.

As I'd predicted, Yngvarr and Badb returned to our palace, but he was, of course, too late to intervene in Fate's plan. Instead, he found our bodies, and I wept with him as he cradled me in his arms and swore he'd get revenge on my behalf. Badb gently pried him away from me, assuring him that when Asgard was safe, my wife and I would receive a proper farewell at sea, but the gods who were responsible for our murders were still in our world. Badb hadn't forgotten her promise to me, and it was only then she told my brother what I'd asked of her a long time ago.

"I have to find his sword," she said. "You make sure Astrid and Áki are all right. Odin must know one of Havard's children or grandchildren will inherit the Sword of Asgard. Make sure they're protected. I *will* retrieve Havard's sword, and for now, I'll take it back to the Otherworld until Astrid tells us what she wants us to do with it."

"All right," Yngvarr whispered. "This is Odin's doing. My brother—"

"Justice will be done," Badb interrupted. "Don't do anything stupid, Yngvarr. Be careful."

She kissed him quickly then left to find Dagan, who'd carried the Sword of Asgard away. Yngvarr clenched his teeth and turned on his heels, heading toward Valaskjalf where I suspected he had every intention of doing something stupid. But Áki caught up to him first, grabbing his arm and stopping him to ask, "Astrid's parents?"

Yngvarr only shook his head.

"You're going to confront Odin then?" Áki asked.

"No," Yngvarr hissed. "I'm going to kill him."

"I'm coming with you."

I wanted to shout at them to listen to Badb, to keep their senses and not make things worse for all of Asgard or to lose their lives in the process of seeking vengeance too soon. But I no longer had a voice, and they marched onward until they reached the edge of Valhalla where a troop of Odin's warriors stopped them. I braced myself for the inevitable fight and the possibility of seeing my brother and son-in-law killed, but one of the warriors simply looked at Yngvarr and said, "Odin is expecting you."

"I'm sure he is," Yngvarr answered.

The warriors led them to Valaskjalf where Odin sat on his throne, impatiently tapping his fingers on the armrest as if he'd been kept waiting. Yngvarr immediately drew his sword and stepped forward, but Odin lifted his hand and warned him, "You may wish to learn why I asked my warriors to allow you inside."

Áki grabbed Yngvarr's arm and whispered, "He knows no boundaries and respects no laws. Take care here."

Odin smiled, but it was a sinister smile, a grin of hatred and malice toward the man who'd shown him he'd lost the respect and allegiance of so many in Asgard, even among the Valkyries. But his smile faded as a warrior burst into the room and ran to his side, bowing before his king as he told him, "My lord, we just found Dagan's body. The sword is missing."

Odin rose from his throne and thundered, "Where is my sword?"

"*Your* sword has not been taken," Yngvarr sneered. "But my brother's sword has been safely transported to the Otherworld where *you* will never be welcomed, which means it is forever out of your reach. And one day, its rightful heir will claim it and take his place on that throne."

Odin shouted numerous curses at Yngvarr and Áki and our entire family and knocked over a statue of his father that stood next to his throne. It shattered against the floor, but in Odin's rage, he didn't seem to notice. And Yngvarr and Áki just stood there, satisfied by his anger and frustration that Badb had bested him. But I didn't want to witness this scene any longer, because I just *knew* it would end badly for my brother and son-in-law. How could it not?

There was no way to escape it though. And as Odin

collected his wrath and calmed his temper, he narrowed his eyes at Áki and that sinister smile returned. "Leave this world," he said. "Take your family and go back to Midgard where you belong."

Áki and Yngvarr exchanged a worried glance. What kind of trickery was this?

My confusion gave way to understanding: Odin didn't yet know who the rightful heir to Asgard's throne would be. None of us knew because he hadn't yet been born. The only way to protect his throne was to allow that heir to claim the sword, to identify himself as the next king of Asgard, and to murder him, too. And the sword itself would have to be discarded, destroyed... or handed over to a god whose magic could change its purpose.

But even if Yngvarr or Áki figured out the reason for Odin's offer, they could hardly refuse it. Áki had the chance to keep his family safe, to ensure their survival in the world where he'd been born. They could live normal lives, and have their own families, and maybe, one day, his descendants could return to Asgard. And he *had* once promised me that was exactly what he'd do.

Áki had just agreed to leave with Astrid and their children when everyone sensed something changing in Asgard, as if the air itself was spreading confusion among the gods and warriors and Valkyries and all who lived inside those walls. And as the air settled, returning to its normalcy, only Odin remembered why Yngvarr stood before him and why parts of Asgard were burning and bodies littered the battlefield of Valhalla.

Because Freyja's curse had fallen on Asgard, and I'd been erased from the pages of its story.

CHAPTER NINETEEN

Grande Terre was simply a largely deserted island again, all vestiges of Sumer III vanishing as soon as the dust settled from Ninurta's storm and death. I scanned the survivors for Keira and found her helping one of her sisters to her feet. Yngvarr ran his fingers through his sandy blond hair and let out a slow breath as he surveyed the damage with me.

"Zababa?" I asked.

"Dead," he assured me.

"Havard showed me..." I trailed off because I could so easily recall how painful it had been for him to see his brother weeping and clutching his body, which meant it hurt *me* now to think about it.

Yngvarr kept his eyes on Agnes who was helping Nuada to his feet. He looked injured but not gravely so. "Zababa held the Sword of Asgard, but he's not the only one who killed my brother."

"I know," I said. "And he's been waiting over thirty years for the chance to kill me."

Yngvarr nodded and finally looked at me, checking for

any signs of injury, but miraculously, I was fine. "What now?" he asked.

I gestured toward Enki who remained standing but had been surrounded by Valkyries who were awaiting orders. But not just any orders—they were waiting on *mine*.

"What about Ninhursag?" I asked Yngvarr.

"Agnes killed her," he answered. "The only magic left on Grande Terre is Freyja's."

I narrowed my eyes at Enki who'd allowed us to live once and called out to him, "Regretting not killing me when you had the chance, aren't you?"

Enki smirked and shrugged. "You'll still die, Gavyn. There's no escaping destiny."

"Yeah," I agreed. "I guess that means dying here was always yours." To the small group of Valkyries keeping him prisoner, I added, "Kill him."

By the time I retuned my attention to Keira, she'd knelt on the ground by the body of one her sisters. I could see her shoulders shaking as she cried and left my great-uncle's side to comfort her, even though offering comfort wasn't exactly my forte.

It wasn't until I was right behind her that I recognized the fallen Valkyrie on the ground as the beautiful blonde who'd flirted with me in the conference room in Reykjavik, which had annoyed the hell out of Keira though I hadn't been able to figure out why. I didn't know yet that they were sisters, and I certainly didn't believe they were Valkyries, demigoddesses who roamed ancient battlefields and escorted the bravest warriors to Odin's hall.

"Róta," I breathed.

Heidi sat beside Keira, holding a bloody hand to her side and stroking her dead sister's hair with the other.

"Keira, I..." But I was speechless once again, voiceless in this ocean of tragedy. All around me, people were mourning losses on both sides, but death didn't care if we were Norse or Sumerian or Irish. In the end, we all died the same.

"Gavyn?" Yngvarr said.

I glanced over my shoulder where Yngvarr had stooped beside a lifeless body lying face down on the rocky terrain of Grande Terre. I'd walked right past him without registering who this body had belonged to, but now I noticed the bow still clutched in his left hand.

"Ull," I sighed.

Yngvarr nodded and touched the god's neck, feeling for a pulse, but it was just an automatic reaction. He couldn't possibly believe there was any hope that Ull was actually alive.

At the other end of the battlefield, Frey and Freyja quickly hugged one another as they ascertained each was relatively unscathed then they went about the tedious task of forcing the surrendering Sumerian demigods into one area so we could decide what we'd do with them. I caught Joachim helping another Valkyrie to her feet, but she was reluctant to leave a fallen sister.

"I'm going to help Nuada get home," Agnes announced. "I'll be back soon, and we'll figure out what to do next."

I nodded but my attention had returned to Keira who was becoming increasingly agitated by Heidi's refusal to abandon their deceased sisters and seek medical help.

"We'll come back for them," Keira promised. "But you're hurt, and I *will* get you to a doctor, even if I have to knock you out first."

"That's probably not a good idea," I said helpfully.

Keira glared at me so I shrugged and said, "Adding a concussion to her list of injuries won't help."

"Come on," Freyja said, leaving the Sumerian demigods under the supervision of her brother and Joachim. "I'll make sure you get the wounded Valkyries to a hospital."

Keira seemed surprised by her offer, but Heidi didn't argue with the goddess. After lifting her onto one of the winged horses, Keira grabbed my shoulders and pulled me within inches of her face. "Promise me you'll wait for me to return and won't do anything stupid."

How could she ask *me* of all people not to do anything stupid? When Agnes had warned Yngvarr of the same thing, it had made sense because Yngvarr was... well, *smart*. Seriously, sometimes they acted like they didn't even *know* me.

"I promise I'll try not to," I said.

"Gavyn," she sighed.

"Keira, you know that's the most honest promise I can make."

She thought about it and sighed again. "You'd better try *really* hard." She kissed me then climbed onto the horse, and several of them took to the air, carrying the wounded Valkyries and their escorts who were ensuring they reached the hospital safely to... I'd never even asked *where* they were going, considering we were in the south Indian Ocean and there was a reason these islands were known as *Desolation* Islands.

"I suppose we need to figure out what to do with our prisoners," Yngvarr said.

"I think we should hand them over to Marduk."

He arched an eyebrow at me as if questioning why Fate would've chosen *me* of all heroes to wield this sword, but I waved him off. "We can't become prison guards, and they've surrendered so it's not right to just kill them. Turn them over to the god who will lead their pantheon now and let him decide what to do with them."

"All right," he agreed reluctantly. "But, seriously, if Marduk comes back with an army of heroes and—"

I snorted and put my hand on his shoulder. "Then we defeat them again, Uncle."

"That had better not become a thing," he mumbled.

"What?" I asked innocently. "Defeating Sumerian armies or calling you Uncle? I mean, you *are* my uncle, right?"

Yngvarr almost smiled, but considering we were surrounded by death and misery, we weren't really in the joking mood, and I dropped the whole smartass nephew thing as we moved our dead to one area so they could be brought home as soon as Asgard's fate was settled.

Agnes returned from the Otherworld and assured us Nuada would be fine then she and Yngvarr began to plot ways to determine if Odin was on Earth still, but I largely ignored them. I had no intention of plotting *anything* or leaving this stupid, rocky island until Keira returned. I kept myself busy watching the sky for approaching jet-horses, and by the time I spotted them, Agnes and Yngvarr had basically come up with war plans for every conceivable scenario, including a surprise Canadian invasion of the U.S., which I was pretty sure was just because they were bored, but I wasn't ruling out an actual Canadian sneak attack. I wasn't really sure *what* that had to do with us, but if I were a war god intent on taking over a country to then attempt ruling the world, Canada would be the way to go: no one would suspect it. And, really, that was probably Ninurta's biggest mistake: he'd aimed too high too soon.

But as the winged horses drew nearer, I realized something was wrong.

Four had left this island, but only three were returning.

Agnes must've noticed, too, because she tried to reassure me by saying, "One of them probably stayed behind at the hospital. They wouldn't just leave their sisters alone."

I nodded because that made total sense. Of course they'd want someone with the wounded Valkyries. But the hollow feeling in my stomach wouldn't leave, and I refused to look away from the winged horses dipping lower in the sky, descending toward the island. I tried to make out their riders, but apparently, being a demigod and heir to a magical sword hadn't granted me Superman vision. But Keira had insisted she'd return, had begged me to promise her I'd wait for her and not do anything stupid. She wouldn't have volunteered to stay with her sisters, so she *had* to be among them.

By the time I could make out who was returning, the winged horses were preparing to land, and that hollow feeling in my stomach had ignited into a fire threatening to consume me.

Keira wasn't among them.

Freyja's horse landed first, and she quickly slid off and met my gaze, but her expression told me everything I feared was true.

"Where is she?" I asked, but my voice didn't sound like my own. It was distant and small and maybe I'd only imagined I'd asked her aloud but the words were stuck in my mind.

"My spell," she replied. "I told you it couldn't hide us forever."

"Freyja, *where is she?*" I yelled.

"Odin took her!" she yelled back. "I don't know how he got to that hospital so quickly, but he was waiting for us as we left and—"

"And you didn't protect her?" I interrupted. The sword in my hand burned brightly, but it paled in comparison to the burning within me.

"We tried," she snapped. "It's *Odin*, Gavyn. He caught us off guard then crossed the veil. We could've followed him to Asgard and gotten ourselves killed or come back here to tell you since you have the only weapon powerful enough to kill a god like him."

I spun around and grabbed Yngvarr's arm, demanding, "Take me to Asgard."

"Gavyn—"

"Goddamn it, Yngvarr, take me to Asgard!" I shouted.

A part of some tiny piece of my brain that was still capable of thinking rationally realized that Yngvarr most likely wanted to talk to Agnes and Freyja, these brilliant goddesses of war, so the three of them could come up with a rescue mission that might actually work. But we all knew why he'd taken Keira, and why I had to go to Asgard now.

Perhaps the power of the Sword of Asgard was also its curse. Those who were able to wield its power were condemned to die by its blade in order to save the ones they loved. And honestly, we should've known this ending was coming, that ultimately, my prophecy and Keira's that had been inextricably linked from the beginning were woven together by the sword and the god who was responsible for my great-grandfather's murder.

And, surely, Yngvarr knew it, too. So I was somewhat surprised when the cold, desolate island dissolved into the warm beauty of Asgard, with Valhalla's golden spires gleaming in the sunlight and its verdant fields teeming with gods and goddesses and Odin's warriors. They weren't yet fighting, but clearly, the tension had returned when Freyja's curse was broken. But without an apparent heir to the throne, those who opposed Odin's rule didn't seem to know what to do.

The Sword of Light alerted them all to my presence because it outshone Asgard's sun as I walked toward Valaskjalf. But in order to reach Odin's palace, I would have to go through Valhalla, and Odin's slain and risen warriors had no intention of allowing me to pass.

The first to reach me, perhaps twenty of them, would never rise again. As the Sword of Light passed through them, they disintegrated, leaving nothing behind to rise at the end of the day. Whispers and murmurs spread through the battlefield as a dozen more fighters attempted to stop me but met the same fate. And it was only then the army of Valhalla slowly began to realize they wouldn't be able to stop me. And I would destroy every last one of them to get to Keira and save her life.

Not all of Odin's soldiers died that day. Some retreated as I crossed the border between Valhalla and Valaskjalf and none attempted to follow me beyond the battlefield. But I never reached Odin's palace, because the god of war was waiting for me outside, my Valkyrie on her knees before him with Áki's sword at her throat.

And it was just like that bastard to threaten her life with the sword my family had once given the boy Keira had raised. We really had come full circle.

"This is where your story ends, Gavyn," Odin said. "Where you make a choice: your life or hers."

"Don't," Keira begged me.

I refused to meet her eyes. I refused to let her beg me to choose my life over hers.

"She's your *daughter*," I said, as if he'd simply forgotten the Valkyries were his own children. And his laughter told me what a ridiculous thing it had been to say.

"I was wrong," she cried. "It was my father the entire time."

Her prophecy. How she'd begged me not to trade my life for hers when I fought Ninurta. She'd assumed the Sumerian god of war would be the one to press a sword to her throat, to demand I sacrifice myself for her or watch her die, but yeah... she'd been wrong. It had always been her father we should've worried about the most.

Odin pressed my grandfather's sword closer to her throat, drawing a thin line of bright red blood, but Keira wouldn't cry out or acknowledge fear or pain. She wanted me to live. She wanted me to choose to fight.

And I would disappoint her for the last time.

"All right," I said, still *hoping* that as soon as I died, the sword's power would transfer to Yngvarr and he could avenge my death as well as his brother's. He hadn't followed me through Valhalla, but he most likely wasn't far away. Maybe he could retrieve the sword before Odin disappeared with it. "We both know it's not really the sword you've wanted but me. Give me your word you'll let her live, and you can have my life."

"No!" Keira screamed, but Odin had already moved the blade farther from her throat and held her still so she couldn't take this choice away from me, so she couldn't take my place.

"She's no threat to me," he said. "I'd have no reason to kill her. You have my word."

I took a deep breath and wondered why Havard had been so silent all this time, if he'd abandoned me or if by sharing his last memory with me, by finishing his own story, his spirit was finally at peace. Maybe he didn't even know what I was thinking or what I was about to do. But even if he did, how could he tell me to act differently when he'd done the same thing to save my mother?

"Okay," I agreed. "My life for hers." I finally lowered my eyes and met hers and even as she continued to beg me to change my mind, I told her, "I love you more than anything, more than everything."

"No sword is worth her life."
"But is she worth yours?" he asked.
"She is worth everything," I answered without hesitation.

I knelt on the ground in front of them and propped the Sword of Asgard in the grass, pointing the tip toward my heart, and took a deep breath before throwing myself onto the blade and fulfilling my own prophecy.

CHAPTER TWENTY

I thought death wouldn't hurt. I mean, it shouldn't, right? Or maybe I was taking too long to die, and somehow, I'd managed to screw up even my own death. Because my chest *hurt* even though I couldn't move, and Asgard had become dark and cold and soundless. My second thought was that if *this* was my eternal reward for saving the world, I needed to have a serious talk with whatever god had made *that* decision.

But for the first time since telling me about his own death, Havard spoke to me. And I'd never been so glad to hear his voice, to know I wasn't alone after all.

"Gavyn, I don't know how to tell you this, but... I don't think you're actually dead."

"So I did screw this up," I sighed. *"I really am the King of Village Idiots."*

"No. The sword pierced your heart. You can't possibly be alive either."

I sighed even louder—not literally, of course, considering my body was now useless—and snapped, *"What kind of mythological bullshit is this? How can I not be dead or alive?"*

"Um... I actually have no idea."

"*You're as helpful as ever*," I muttered.

And then I heard her voice, that gentle sound that rolled off her tongue like a lullaby no matter what she was saying, even if she was scolding me for spilling grape juice on her bone white tablecloth. "Grandpa, may I ride Sigurd again? Can he take me to Midgard?"

"*Havard*," I whispered. "*Stop it.*"

She wasn't really with me in Asgard or wherever I was now, of course, because my mother had died fifteen years before. It was a memory of her as a child, begging her grandfather to ride his favorite stallion to a world she hadn't yet adopted as her own.

But Havard whispered back, "*Gavyn, I'm not controlling it. I don't even remember this.*"

My mom turned her face up toward her grandfather, and he smiled down at her and lifted her onto Sigurd's back. "You may ride but only in Asgard."

"But why, Grandpa? Why can't I go to Midgard?"

"Because as long as Odin is gone, you're safe here."

"And he's in Midgard?"

"I don't know where he is, but just in case, I'd rather you stay here where your family can watch over you. Don't you know how precious you are to all of us?"

My mom thought about it and decided, "I'm not afraid of him. And I won't let him hurt you either, Grandpa."

Havard laughed and said, "You are as brave as the fiercest warrior in Valhalla. But one day a very long time from now, he will return. And when that day comes, you have to escape. You have your own destiny to fulfill, Hjordis. You're not only precious to us but to every god in Asgard because of who you will bring into our world."

She stubbornly shook her head and insisted, "I want us to be together forever. I can get married and have kids here, just like Grandma and Mama."

Havard smiled and assured her, "We *will* be together forever. We are a part of one another, and I will always be there within you if you only search for me."

"Forever?" she asked.

"Forever," he promised.

My mom looked skeptical as she squinted down at him, but she also seemed to be processing this promise and trying to make sense of it. "It isn't right, Grandpa. It isn't right that Odin should get to live and come back to rule here when he does such terrible things."

Havard patted Sigurd's neck and nodded. "It isn't, but Fate has a way of balancing the universe and ensuring what is evil is always punished. And I've told you before, Granddaughter. I won't *really* die. I'll live on in your son, and he will inherit all of my power and wield this sword, and he will one day rule the gods as I would have. And I know this because the Sword of Prophecy has shown it to me."

"And will I live forever in him, too?" she asked.

"Yes," he answered. "Death can never separate those who love one another."

I interrupted Havard's memory, which he'd claimed he wasn't forcing me to relive, to chastise him for it. Did he really think I wasn't in enough pain, and I needed my heart figuratively broken as well as literally? "*I told you to knock it off. As soon as I'm done dying, I will find you and kick your ass.*"

But it wasn't Havard's voice that answered me. "*Death can never separate those who love one another. I love you, Gavyn.*"

And strangely, it seemed as if my heart began to beat again as I whispered back, "*I love you, too, Mom.*" The burning pain in my chest vanished and my world filled with light and sounds and smells. But my initial belief that I'd somehow been lucky enough to sneak into Heaven vanished as well when I felt someone trying to pry my sword from my hand.

I opened my eyes and stared at a surprised god of war who

knew I should be dead, but somehow, I'd defied death. Odin recoiled, mumbling, "How?" to himself, but I was far less concerned with *how* I was alive than claiming what rightly belonged to me and Yngvarr and my mother and Arnbjorg, and most of all, Havard.

It didn't even occur to me, not right away, that Asgard seemed just a little bit different, that I *thought* about Odin and this battle and the potential war that could ensue just a little differently, too.

As I rose from the ground still stained with my blood, I flipped the Sword of Asgard over in my hand to grasp the hilt and caught my symbol engraved in the silver. But it was no longer just an emblem representing my name. Beneath it were new words, an inscription. *God of War*.

I looked up at Odin who still held Áki's sword and for the first time, noticed Keira had been beside me all along. Her neck was still bleeding and even though it wasn't a serious injury, it was the last one Odin would inflict on us. I advanced, but he deflected my attack. I swung my sword again, catching his right wrist as he attempted to retreat. Somehow, this legendary god of war managed to catch Áki's sword with his left hand as his right fell to the ground.

"Did you really think you could escape your own fate?" I asked him. "That you'd never have to atone for Havard's murder?"

"Do *you* really think I wouldn't do it again?" he replied. "You only know his side of the story. What makes you think he hasn't lied to you, just as he once lied to all of Asgard?"

"Because I know it's his truth," I said. "Those are my memories, and I know they're *our* truth."

Odin gritted his teeth and advanced on me, albeit somewhat awkwardly since he'd lost his dominant hand. If he'd been any other god, I may have pitied him. If he'd begged for mercy, I may have even granted it, brought him to his knees and accepted a surrender rather than running my sword through his other arm, ensuring he couldn't fight back before telling this god who'd taken so much from us, "I hope you burn in Hell."

And the Sword of Asgard that had carried his name for over a thousand years took his life, finishing this chapter of Asgard's story and beginning a new one, a blank page that would start with my name.

I CROSSED my arms and glared at the massive seat in front of me. "I *still* think it's awfully ostentatious."

"How many times do we have to tell you not to use big words?" Agnes teased. "You know it freaks us out."

"You don't have to stay here," Yngvarr reminded me. "My home is yours."

I pretended to gag and said, "No way. I'm not living in a witch's sex palace."

Instead of scolding me for calling her a witch for the millionth time, Agnes just smiled and shrugged. "Don't blame you."

"I think we should destroy it," Keira announced. The scar on her throat was hardly visible now, but I would always know it was there, a permanent reminder of the kind of god I'd never become. If the power bestowed on me ever tempted me to lead Asgard astray, I'd only have to trace my finger across that small, white line and remember how close I'd come to losing everything that mattered.

"Well, you and Keira can't stay at her place forever," Yngvarr argued.

"Why not?" I argued back. "Dad decided to go back home, and Hunter's dumb ass turned me down, too. Grandma and Grandpa didn't want to return because my uncles have families and they're all happy there. So it's not like we *need* a lot of space." I winked at Keira and added, "At least until we have our own kids to run wild through Asgard."

I thought she blushed a little, but she also smiled as she pictured that future with me.

"Yeah, but it's not exactly a home for a god, let alone the one ruling Asgard," Yngvarr said. "Just because you freed the Valkyries from their servitude doesn't mean you should prove how different you are than your predecessor by living like—"

"Might want to reconsider however you're planning on finishing that sentence," Keira warned.

Yngvarr grinned sheepishly at her and said, "I just think he should live like the ruler of Asgard."

I blinked at him before snapping, "What does that even *mean?*"

"I think he's implying he wants us to move into Valaskjalf," Keira supplied helpfully.

Yngvarr nodded and said, "Listen to your wife. She's way smarter than you."

So I snickered and agreed with him. "I plan to. And not just about this but pretty much everything." And because Yngvarr was right, and Keira *was* way smarter than me, I put my arm around her and kissed the side of her head, deciding, "We're tearing this whole place down, not just the throne. I don't want anyone to have to look at this palace anymore. We won't erase Odin from our history, but no one will ever sit on his throne again."

Yngvarr smiled and gave up. "Well, I think that's what Havard would've wanted anyway."

"Yeah," I agreed. "That's exactly how he wants our story to begin."

THE END

Thank you for reading the *Heroes of Asgard* series. If you've enjoyed my humorous take on world mythology, you might enjoy *The Unbreakable Sword* series, which is also filled with smartass demigods, deities from multiple world pantheons, and yet another missing sword.

MYTHOLOGY GLOSSARY

If Gavyn gives one of the characters a nickname, I've put it in parentheses right after his or her actual name

Aesir—one of the two tribes of gods in Norse mythology, and the tribe associated with most of the Norse gods such as Odin, Thor, and Tyr. The other tribe is the Vanir.

Anhur—Egyptian god of war who was sometimes portrayed with the head of a lion, which is why he can shift into a lion in this series.

Anubis—in Egyptian mythology, Anubis is a god of the dead and is associated with jackals.

Arnbjorg—isn't a real mythological figure; I made her up for this story. She is the love interest of Havard.

Asalluhi—Mesopotamian god of incantations and magic.

Asgard—the realm of the Aesir, one of the two races of gods

in Norse mythology. The other is the Vanir (who originally lived in Vanaheim).

Badb (Agnes)—Irish goddess of war. One of the triune of goddesses who form the Morrigna.

Belatu-Cadros—Celtic god of war. His name is also given as Belatucadros.

Book of Enoch—One of my favorite sources for creating fantasy stories (in fact, it inspired *The Immortals* series), the *Book of Enoch* is a Judeo-Christian text that is non-canonical in most Judeo-Christian religions (with the exceptions of Beta Israel and the Ethiopian Orthodox Tewahedo Church and Eritrean Orthodox Tewahedo Church). What I've always found fascinating about these passages are those specifically referencing the fall of the Watchers, angels who left Heaven to take human wives. With them, they fathered the Nephilim —half angel, half human "giants" who spread all sorts of disaster on Earth until God sent a flood and wiped them out (as well as the other humans who'd been taught warfare and all sorts of things they weren't supposed to be doing because of those pesky, horny angels).

Cerberus—in Greek mythology, Cerberus was the original Hellhound who guarded the gates of Hades to prevent all those poor bastards from leaving. He's often depicted as having multiple heads (usually three), and sometimes, as having snakes protruding from his body. Seriously: the easiest way to ensure something is terrifying as all Hell is to throw snakes into the mix.

Dagan—a Mesopotamian fertility god. There's really not

much else out there about him, which is cool... he's only in this book to get killed anyway.

Dante's *Inferno* and the Nine Circles of Hell—Dante Alighieri was a fourteenth century Italian poet who is most famous for his *Divine Comedy*. Divided into three parts, the first describes his journey through Hell, which is recreated in this book as a trap for Gavyn and his allies. Since numerous monsters and gods await them, just as they awaited Dante, I'll briefly recap the nine circles here.

> 1. *Limbo*. This first circle is for those without sin, but who were not Christians. This isn't really a circle of torment as the others, but rather a dull and dreary place.
> 2. *Lust*. The second circle is guarded by Minos, the mythological king of Crete (see his entry for more information on him). In Dante's poem, he is turned into a serpent man (torso of a man, lower body of a serpent). It is his eternal punishment to condemn those who enter Hell to a particular circle, which he determines by wrapping his tail around their bodies. Depending on the number of times his tail goes around the body, that is the corresponding circle that person is condemned to. In this story, he just attacks Gavyn and his pals. What a swell guy.
> 3. *Gluttony*. The third circle is nasty. Like *seriously* gross. It has this perpetually vile, putrid, icy rain that turns the streets to slush, and to make it even *more* fun, Cerberus roams the streets with his almost equally vile, nasty snake body.
> 4. *Greed*. The fourth circle is filled with people weighted down by enormous stones and is guarded by

Plutus, the Greek god of wealth (see his entry for more information).

5. *Wrath*. The fifth circle is located in the swampy waters of Styx. People were condemned to fight atop the swamp (don't have a clue how *that* was possible), while Phlegyas (who also has his own entry in this glossary) served as the transport across Styx to the inner circles of Hell (the area inside the final wall is known as the City of Dis and its walls are guarded by fallen angels, which I describe in the book).

6. *Heresy*. This is where Gavyn confronts the fallen angels outside the walls of the City of Dis. I've roughly based those angels on the *Book of Enoch* (which I've described above). He can see the fires raging within from the swampy area in the sixth circle. Here, I've taken more liberties than usual with the source material, because I moved all those fires inside the walls. In Dante's *Inferno*, the people condemned to this circle are suffering in fiery tombs.

7. *Violence*. The seventh circle is divided into three rings. The first is a river of boiling blood and fire and is guarded by centaurs. The second is filled with woods and harpies. And the third is a plain of burning sand and fiery rain. Between the seventh and eighth circles is Geryon (described in his entry).

8. *Fraud*. Large ditches and sharp stones fill the eighth circle, which is guarded by horned demons, monstrous reptiles, diseases, and darkness. Spoiler alert if you're reading this before the novel: we don't actually find out what happens to all the Houstonians who'd been infected with the plague. I'd like to think they survived, so surely, that counts for something, right?

9. *Treachery*. The ninth and final circle is an icy lake

with a central well (technically, it's at the bottom of the central well where the ninth circle lays and where the Devil himself is spending his eternal punishment). The other four rings are named for notorious biblical traitors like Cain and Judas.

Enki—Sumerian god of magic and wisdom, and father of Marduk and Asalluhi. His Babylonian counterpart, Ea, was regarded as the creator and protector of humanity. Because he's associated with Ninhursag in Sumerian myths, they are married in this story.

Forseti—in Norse mythology, he is a god of justice. The only mention of him in the *Poetic Edda* discusses his home and identifies him as someone who settles disputes. I've made him the mediator in this series as well.

Frey—Norse god of prosperity, fertility, and peace. He and his sister, Freyja, are members of the Vanir and were brought to Asgard to live among the Aesir when the war between the two tribes ended.

Freyja—Norse goddess of love, sex, fertility, and war. Known for her unparalleled beauty, she's often coveted by different gods and mythological figures, while she tends to covet jewelry, particularly Brísingamen (her necklace).

Gerd—gastroesophageal reflux disease. Just making sure you're paying attention. In Norse mythology, she's Frey's wife. Frey saw her from a distance and instantly fell in love with her.

Geryon—in Greek mythology, Geryon is portrayed as a giant

monster with human faces, and quite possibly, a dragon-like body.

Gunnr (Keira)—a Valkyrie. In Norse mythology, Valkyries would select which men would fall in battle and bring them to Valhalla.

Havard—isn't a real mythological figure. He's made up for this story, in which he's a god of war. I know his name is a pain in the ass (trust me: I'm the one who's having to type it), but I chose it because of its meaning. It contains old Norse elements that translate as "high defender" and I thought that was fitting for his character. If it helps, I keep pronouncing it as "Hav-ard."

Heimdall—Norse god whose impeccable sight and hearing make him an excellent watchman for the unfolding of Ragnarok. He also possesses the gift of foresight (ability to foretell future events).

Hildr (Heidi)—one of the Valkyries.

Idun—Norse goddess whose apples grant the gods eternal youth.

Inanna—Sumerian goddess of beauty, love, sex, war, and justice. Yeah, I have no idea why the ancient Sumerians decided to lump all those different characteristics together. Maybe they just ran out of deities.

Inti—in Incan mythology, Inti is a sun god and was one of the most important deities of the Incan civilization.

Kulullû—like a lot of Mesopotamian mythology, we don't

know a lot about these mythical monsters, partly just because their culture is so *old* that we've lost a lot of their records. We do know they were portrayed as "fish-men" and may have been associated with Marduk.

Ljósálfar—in Norse mythology, it is the realm of the "light elves." In this series, it refers to the Norse's name for Ireland.

Ma'at—in Egyptian mythology, she is the daughter of Ra and the goddess associated with balance, truth, justice, and morality. She is often depicted as weighing the worth of deceased mortals and gods by a ceremony in which the person's heart was weighed against a feather. In order to pass into Aaru (the place people *wanted* to go), their heart had to be lighter than her feather. Otherwise, they ended up in Duat (the place no one wanted to go).

Mama Pacha—in Incan mythology, Mama Pacha is an earth and fertility goddess who can cause earthquakes.

Marduk—patron god of Babylon, he is a complex figure associated with magic and incantations, and is often syncretized with Enki and Asalluhi.

Minos—the mythological first King of Crete who would force seven young boys and girls to enter the Labyrinth and get eaten by the Minotaur every seven years. Nice guy, right? But then along comes this hot hero, Theseus, and Ariadne (Minos's daughter) is all like, "Oh, HELLZ yeah!" and the architect of the Labyrinth, Daedalus, gives her a clue as to how Theseus can escape. This pisses off Minos who starts chasing poor Daedalus through Greece and into Sicily, where he finds him at King Cocalus's court. But the king's daughters are protective of the old inventor and basically boil Minos alive while he's taking a bath. So...score one for scorned women. After his death, he becomes one of three judges in Hades.

Morrigna—a triune of Irish war goddesses formed the Morrigna. The three goddesses are usually given as Badb, Macha, and Nemain, although Nemain is sometimes replaced with Morrigan or Anand. Each goddess represents a different aspect of war.

Nergal—ancient Mesopotamian god of war and pestilence who commands a number of demonic entities.

Ninhursag—Sumerian mother goddess who is regarded as a creator of gods and men. She is the mother of Ninurta. Seriously, these family trees are complicated as hell, and Gavyn is more than a little suspicious that this whole war is just a family feud gone nuclear.

Ninurta—another ancient Mesopotamian war god, Ninurta played a small enough role in *The Unbreakable Sword* series to warrant a bigger part in this series. His enchanted weapon, Sharur (sometimes a talking mace, sometimes a talking spear) will be back in book two, but unfortunately, it doesn't talk to Gavyn.

Njord and Skadi—I reference their ill-fated marriage, so here's the gist of the story: Skadi lived in the highest mountain where the snow never melted, and Njord lived on the beach. They loved their homes, and since those homes were completely different, they were miserable whenever they stayed with their spouse. Eventually, they decided to return to their homes separately since neither could be happy in the other's land.

Nótt—personification of night in Norse mythology. She rides a horse across the sky, which drags night behind her.

Nuada—in Irish mythology, Nuada is the leader of the Tuatha Dé who is a great warrior and ruler but loses his right arm in a vicious battle. Since a blemished king couldn't rule, he was forced to give up his throne. The god of healing, Dian Cécht, made Nuada a silver arm but it wasn't enough to get him the throne back, so Dian Cécht's son, Miach, causes skin to grow over the silver appendage, which pisses off his dad because he was all like, "How dare you show me up!" so he kills him. *Kills* him, y'all.

Odin—the All-Father of the Aesir, Odin is one of the most famous gods of Norse mythology. Although he's a war god, Odin is also associated with magic and wisdom. His wife is the goddess, Frigg.

Paricia—an obscure name in Incan mythology, this god may be synonymous with Pacha Kamaq. He is most known for sending a flood to wipe out people who weren't paying him the proper respect. In this series, he is a water deity since he's sent tidal waves to punish people for not submitting.

Phlegyas—best known in Greek mythology for not showing the proper respect to the gods, he's portrayed in Virgil's *Aeneid* as being eternally tormented in Tartarus. This is intended to warn others not to piss off the gods, which always seems like good advice.

Plutus—the Greek god of wealth. Aristophanes kinda turned him into a real douchebag in his plays, because he kinda wreaks havoc in determining who is worthy of wealth and who isn't. But if you think about it, it's also fitting since money is pretty much the root of the vast majority of wars throughout history, so I guess Aristophanes was onto something.

Ra (Most Loathsome God in the Universe)—in Egyptian mythology, Ra is one of the sun gods (specifically, god of the noon sun). He is associated with falcons and is often depicted with the head of a falcon.

Róta—one of the Valkyries.

Sharur—Ninurta's enchanted weapon (either a mace or spear), which could supposedly talk…I'm really not sure what good a talking weapon is.

Sif—in Norse mythology, Sif is Thor's wife. An earth goddess, she is best known for her beautiful blond hair, which Loki infamously cut off as a prank…and not surprisingly, Thor didn't take it too well and threatened to kill him. Loki got away with his life after promising Thor he'd have a golden…wig?…made for her. The same dwarfs who make Sif's new hair make Mjollnir as well as several other gifts for the gods.

Skidbladnir—man, Norse names crack me up. Okay, so this particularly awful one is the name of Frey's magical ship, which could be folded like a napkin and carried around with him. But, hey, size doesn't matter, right? It was also the fastest ship, despite its… oh, wait. Once it was actually being used as a ship, it was also the largest of ships, so I guess size *does* matter.

Supay—in Incan mythology, this god of death rules over

Ukhu Pacha (the underworld) and commands an army of demons. Gavyn is not a fan.

Thor—god of thunder, storms, and fertility, Thor probably shares the top-honor of being the most recognizable Norse god along with his father, Odin. He defends Asgard with his hammer, Mjölnir, and is also known for being a protector of humans.

Tiamat—Babylonian goddess who takes the form of a dragon to battle Marduk. She's just a dragon in this story and not a very nice one.

Tova—not a real Norse goddess. I made her up for this story, in which she's the daughter of Freyja.

Tuatha Dé—the gods of Irish mythology. Also known as the Tuatha Dé Danaan, which means "tribe of (the goddess) Danu."

Tyr—Norse god of war who lost his right hand when he put it in a wolf's (Fenrir's) mouth so he could be restrained. So look: Fenrir would only allow himself to be restrained if some dumbass stuck a hand in his mouth because he suspected the fetter the gods had brought was enchanted. And Tyr was apparently that dumbass. I mean, the gods *did* bind the wolf that was prophesied to be such a terror, and *supposedly* he's gonna stay bound until Ragnarok just like his dad, Loki (yeah, because Norse mythology is F.R.E.A.K.Y y'all), but he'll just break free then and kill Odin anyway, so what was the point?

Ull—Norse god associated with archery. Not much is known about him, but it's always good to have expert archers on your side.

Valaskjalf—one of Odin's halls. While Valhalla is the hall associated with his dead warriors, Valaskjalf is where he watches over all the realms.

Valhalla—one of Odin's halls. Famously portrayed as having a golden roof, slain warriors are brought to Valhalla by Odin's Valkyries. Here, they fight each day in preparation for Ragnarok and those who fall again rise each night when they all dine with Odin himself. Peachy afterlife, huh?

Vanir—one of the two tribes of Norse gods, the other being the Aesir. Frey and Freyja are from the Vanir.

Vigrid—field on which many battles of Ragnarok are prophesied to occur.

Yngvarr—doesn't exist in Norse mythology; I made him up for this story. Brother of Havard and also a god of war.

Zababa—ancient Mesopotamian war god.

ALSO BY S.M. SCHMITZ

Sign up for my mailing list, which will keep you up to date on new releases and great deals when I put books on sale, here.

For more information, please visit my website at smschmitz.com.

Other titles by S.M. Schmitz

Shadows of the Gods, book one of *The Unbreakable Sword* series (fantasy & mythology)

As a powerful demigod, Selena has been running from the gods who control the government agency, the New Pantheon, for the past three years, but now, they've caught up to her.

When they trap Selena in an alleyway in New Orleans, she is ready to admit defeat. But an unfamiliar demigod rescues her, and the more she learns about Cameron, the more she discovers their common bonds may be the key to unraveling her own mysterious history.

In the first book of The Unbreakable Sword series, Selena and Cameron must not only evade the New Pantheon, which is ruthlessly hunting the remaining gods and their descendants, but an angry Aztec god that wants Selena's power to himself. And they will discover in the impending final battle of the gods, no one can be trusted.

Blades of Ash, an *Unbreakable Sword* series prequel

When Olympus is destroyed, the Tuatha Dé and their Greek

allies want revenge. But what their vengeance costs may haunt them forever.

Badb, one of the triune of Irish war goddesses known as the Mórrígna, is having a rough millennium: the mortals of Ireland have turned away from the Tuatha Dé, and now, the Sumerians have launched a disastrous invasion into Olympus.

Worse, the reason for the invasion isn't as straightforward as they first thought. With powerful players stoking the flames between the Irish alliance and their enemies, both sides may ultimately lose everything, including their own worlds.

The *Resurrected* trilogy, a science-fiction romance (also available in *The Complete Resurrected Trilogy Box Set*)

Awakened from death. Herself but no longer alone in her own body. Two lives merged into one.

A mistake. An aberration. A miracle.

And a company that wants her dead for existing.

When Dietrich's fiancée, Lottie, is killed in a car accident, he descends into his own personal Hell until he runs into her in a café two years later. Claiming she isn't really Lottie but only possesses some of her memories, the young woman offers him an unbelievable story then disappears.

Using his position as a CIA agent to track her down, Dietrich quickly discovers Lottie remembers far more about her past life than she'd originally let on. But his attempt to learn more about the planet she comes from or the woman she is now is disrupted by a group of men from the company that transports people from their home planet to Earth when they find out about her resurrection and attempt to murder her.

Because for Lottie, something went wrong, and her existence threatens their entire business on Earth. And Dietrich's ultimate second chance with the only woman he's ever loved will be threatened as well.

The Chosen, a *Resurrected* series novel

They promised her happily ever after. Instead, they gave her Hell. Now, she's getting revenge.

When Bella agreed to travel to Earth to start a new life with the man she loved, she'd been promised two things: healing dead human bodies so they could live on this planet always worked, and they could have the happily ever after forbidden to them at home.

But soon after arriving on her new planet, she discovers both of those promises were lies. And the consequences for trusting the wrong people are deadly.

After six years of hiding from the company that helped her cross over, she is approached by a beautiful but mysterious stranger who offers her a different kind of promise: the chance for revenge. And Bella's journey to end her own nightmare and to seek justice for the man she'd once loved is finally able to begin.

The Immortals series, a fantasy & mythology series (also available in *The Complete Immortals Series Box Set*)

When demons refuse to play by the rules, all Hell will break loose.

Colin and Anna have been hunting demons for a long time. But something is different in Baton Rouge. The rules are being broken and they're powerless against some of the greatest forces Hell can assemble. If they can't stop these demons from manipulating every rule of this war, then Heaven may lose the only battle that's ever really mattered.

The Golden Eagle, a romantic suspense

After a vicious second civil war in the U.S., the states that seceded are occupied, and the people there live by different rules.

Jon is the highest-ranking officer in an elite Task Force whose purpose is shrouded in mystery. Ava is just trying to survive the occupation after two years of brutal war. After meeting unexpectedly, they discover they are both willing to risk everything for the chance to love one another. But what those risks entail may be far greater than anything either could have imagined.

The Cambria Code series, a science-fiction romance

When a mysterious spaceship appears above Cambria, Zoe remains skeptical that it's anything but an elaborate hoax. By the time the first spaceship is joined by two others, Zoe reluctantly admits that Earth has been invaded, even though it's a pretty lame invasion: the aliens look remarkably human and keep to themselves. From what humans are able to learn about them, they seem incredibly arrogant and boring anyway.

After meeting Peyton, one of Earth's newest residents, Zoe feels an immediate attraction to him although she is reluctant to become involved with someone who isn't even human. But she soon discovers that these aliens are far more dangerous than they've led everyone to believe, and the secrets they are hiding may signal the destruction of her entire planet.

The Scavengers, a post-apocalyptic novella

When nothing is left, what will you treasure most?

In a world completely destroyed by adults, eleven-year-old Nic believes he is the only thing still alive after four years of isolation—the only thing except for the Scavengers.

When he meets Celia, another child in an empty world, they offer one another hope and the promise of an end to the kind of fear and loneliness that only a child abandoned on a dead and forsaken planet could understand.

But Nic's universe, for years centered around Celia, will be tested, and he'll discover just how far he's willing to go to protect them both.

Made in the USA
Monee, IL
19 December 2024

74784732R00132